DRAGON'S KEEP

MAGIC & MECHANICALS BOOK 4

JESSICA MARTING

SHADOW PRESS

Copyright © 2022 J.L. Turner

ISBN 978-1-989780-12-1

Cover art by German Creative

Edited by Christine Kirchoff

CHAPTER 1

8 May 1888

M y dearest Arabella,

Once again, I must implore you to reconsider your ~~foolish foolhardy arse-backwards~~ questionable plan to continue sailing the skies, alone. I acknowledge your considerable experience as an aviator but you must remember that undergoing such journeys across the seas and continents on your lonesome is very dangerous.

I am not explicitly suggesting that you land the dirigible forever, just that you join Clarinda and I for a spell at our home. The weather is lovely in Torquay this time of year, and she has friends she would like to introduce to you. Please consider our invitation.

Much love,
Your devoted father

~

26 May 1888

DEAR FATHER,

I am many years too old for you to go about lying to me. You and Clarinda are scheming to catch a husband for me, and I have made plain my feelings about this fruitless endeavor. Additionally, as someone well-versed in the English climate, the weather in Torquay is not lovely at this time of year, just as it isn't any time of year anywhere in England.

You claim to acknowledge my piloting experience, yet in your next breath proclaim that I'm incapable of plotting journeys successfully sailed by men. You do not fool me, Father.

For the love of all that is holy, do not cross out words in a letter. It is unsightly and unbecoming of the gentleman Clarinda is working so hard to turn you into.

With love,

Arabella

P.S. I do believe you will dearly regret not taking this journey to Antarctica with me.

"ARE YOU INSANE?"

Arabella Greaves fought the uncharacteristic urge in her to fidget or look away from the New York airfield comptroller, whose eyes were nearly bugging out of his head in disbelief.

"No," she said, fighting to keep her voice calm. "I am of sound mind, and I would appreciate your not questioning it." She wanted to point out that the comptroller wouldn't be acting this way had she not been a woman or traveling alone.

"If I may make a suggestion," the comptroller began, but Arabella shook her head, cutting him off.

"You may not. I have twenty-six years of flight experience. I shall be fine on this journey."

He eyed her doubtfully. "You don't look old enough to have been piloting a dirigible for twenty-six years."

Why was this American being so stubborn? "That's how long I've lived on one. I've been aboard dirigibles my entire life!" she snapped. "I started learning to navigate when I was a child, and handling the steering yoke when I was twelve. I've sailed from England to almost everywhere else in the world. I'll be able to handle the distance from New York to Charleston, from Charleston to Havana, Havana to Santiago, and then to Antarctica." She hoped she injected enough of an authoritarian note in her voice to make the comptroller respect her. "I know what I'm doing."

"If you would excuse my impertinence, madam, living aboard a dirigible isn't the same as..."

She cut him off again. "I appreciate your concern, but I will be all right."

"Would you consider joining a group expedition instead?" he asked. The comptroller slid open a drawer of his massive desk behind the flight office counter and removed a sheaf of papers. He slid them across the counter. "This is some information about an upcoming Antarctic dirigible expedition that takes flight in November, so only a few months away. Everyone flies their own dirigible, with radio communication between all vessels and led by three experienced Antarctic guides. There's room for one more dirigible." He looked at her hopefully.

"Why would I want to leave in November?"

"Because it will be spring in the Southern Hemisphere," the comptroller patiently explained. "There will be fewer chances of storms. This is the documentation you need to fill out, and I have more information about the route here."

Arabella hadn't considered the season in the Southern Hemisphere, and immediately felt like an idiot. *Some adventurer I am.* "Of course, but my dirigible has been fully winterized. It will withstand Antarctic conditions this time of year." She pushed the papers back across the counter. "Now, could you please stop fussing over me and let me file my flight plan? I will be leaving this airfield tomorrow morning for Charleston." Keeping her temper in check, she added, "And I will be landing in Antarctica in a few days' time. I've traveled to the Canadian Arctic. I will be able to handle Antarctica."

"I'm sure you have enough experience to pilot a dirigible through severe weather conditions but the Arctic is inhabited by people, and they're very experienced with the climate. Antarctica in the winter is something entirely different. There is nothing and no one there, except for maybe the penguins. People have disappeared when they travel there alone. Didn't you read about that research team a few years back? One of the scientists fell out of the sky."

Arabella's eye twitched at his impertinence. He looked away briefly as he uselessly shuffled the papers she had pushed back at him.

"I won't be making those mistakes. I've already undertaken expeditions to the Ural Mountains, Rocky Mountains, and the Himalayas. Antarctica is the last place on Earth I haven't visited yet, and I fully intend to go on my terms," she said.

"Did you travel to the Himalayas alone?"

A fresh wave of irritation welled in her. "No, I made the journey with my father."

"A trip to Antarctica is a mite more dangerous than the Himalayas. Please understand that I'm not trying to belittle you. I'm genuinely concerned for your wellbeing. I would

4

be trying to talk anyone out of undertaking this without at least a prior trip with experienced guides," the comptroller said. He pushed the papers back across the counter. "Like this one, taking off in November."

"I'm required to be back in England for the Christmas season. My father and his wife have commanded it," Arabella replied stiffly.

"Why not wait until next year? Another expedition leaves in mid-January."

Why was he being so difficult about this? "Could you just file my flight plan?" she snapped. "As I told you, I'll be setting off for Charleston tomorrow morning. I expect that my flight plan will have been received by that comptroller, along with every other airfield comptrollers I'll be seeing by the time I land at each one." She again pushed the papers back across the counter, standing up on her tiptoes to make sure they were as close to the comptroller as possible.

He heaved a gusty sigh. "I'm not going to talk you into a safer route, am I?"

She shook her head.

He reluctantly pushed the papers aside and picked up the form she completed, detailing her flight plan. "I'll send this telegram now. Charleston will be expecting you in a day's time."

~

Five days later

An unearthly gust of wind pushed back Arabella's dirigible, and for a few seconds she was unable to move, frozen in place as she waited to topple over. Flying snow pelted the deck's glass-enclosed flight box where she stood, obscuring her vision. Her efforts were for almost for

5

naught anyway, since there was no sunlight offered in Antarctica at this time of year, and the lights installed on her dirigible's deck were nearly useless in the storm. Fear slammed into her.

She had made the biggest mistake of her life.

A deafening sound above made her raise her head as a cloud of something white, opaque, and floppy fell to the glass ceiling. It took a few seconds for her mind to realize what it was seeing, that the dirigible's balloon had just collapsed on itself.

The dirigible bucked against the wind, warring with it and gravity.

I can fix it. I have a repair kit. I have a helium tank in the hold. I just need to find somewhere to land to conduct the repairs. She repeated the words to herself like a mantra, hoping she was right and she could find somewhere safe to dock her dirigible.

The vessel lurched to the side. She collapsed to the deck and grabbed the steering yoke's base before she could slide away. The wind forced the dirigible upright for a few stable seconds, only to tilt it forward. A crash sounded from the lower deck. Arabella lost her grip on the steering yoke and careened across the interior flight box's polished deck, crashing into its wall.

The flight box's lights flickered and went out.

Unmoored by the total lack of light, Arabella's world seemed to suspend itself in time for a few seconds. She couldn't feel the deck beneath her body or hear the wind and snow pummeling the dirigible.

She didn't regain her senses until the dirigible fell from the sky, when her world ended.

THE SOUND of something hitting the frozen-over ground outside his cave had Xavier wide awake in record time.

What the devil was that?

Curiosity piqued, he got up and tossed aside his makeshift blankets to rise to his feet. Wrapping a blanket around himself to stave off the Antarctic chill, he padded over the cave floor to its mouth and looked outside. Through the swirling snow he could make out the hulking sight of a dirigible, nose-first into the side of the mountain where he'd made his home for the last five years. He could make out the tattered remains of the Union Jack poking out of the snow.

A chill crawled over him in a way that had nothing to do with his surroundings.

A dirigible in this part of the world could mean only one thing: someone had tracked him down and wanted to bring him back to England.

They'll vivisect me!

Terror welled up in him, quickly overridden with determination. He refused to be tortured, to die in the name of scientific advancement. What were the odds that anyone on board survived the crash, anyway?

As he shifted into his beast form, he thought it would be so much easier to just breathe fire on the intruding vessel, to smite it from the face of the earth and pretend it never existed. The storm prevented that from happening, and he wanted to see if there was anything aboard the dirigible that he could use before he destroyed it. There must be treasures aboard that vessel. Excitement bubbled in him at the prospect of plundering it and hoarding everything it contained.

His excitement dimmed when he realized that the dirigible's appearance might mean that people knew of his existence. Another dirigible would appear, and another. He would have to find another cave to live in.

A part of him had always known his hiding place was too good to stay in forever.

The wind and flying snow whipped uselessly at his green scales, heavy and protective as chain mail, as he purposefully made his way through the storm to the fallen dirigible. Its balloon had nearly collapsed on itself, which would partially account for the vessel crashing, and it was deflated against the side of the mountain. As he crawled closer to the dirigible on his clawed feet, he saw that the vessel itself was surprisingly intact. If the balloon could be repaired, the dirigible could fly back to wherever it came from.

His heart sank. That meant there was a chance the dirigible's crew survived.

Xavier hauled himself up the side of the mountain to take a better look. It had an enclosed flight box on the deck, its glass walls already covered in snow and ice, the door frozen shut. Through the glass he could make out a lone figure, crumpled against the wall. When his enhanced vision honed in on the sight, he could make out a long auburn braid beneath a furry hat. Her chest rose and fell steadily, an unwelcome sign of life.

Xavier had never killed anyone before. His chest constricted, thinking about what he had to do if he didn't want anyone to know where he was. Or he could just leave her where she lay, gather his things in his cave, and find somewhere else to hide out if she didn't swiftly succumb to the elements first. Antarctica was a big place. There were bound to be other caves and mountains to hide away in. The idiot who crashed into his mountain would need a repair kit aboard her dirigible, to take care of her damaged balloon. If she could make her way to the Antarctic, she would have the foresight to have repair materials aboard.

But what if she didn't?

Could he live with the knowledge that he condemned someone else to death when he could help keep them alive? He didn't think he could. Indecision warred within him as the wind ripped through his ears and over his scales. What made his decision for him was the reminder that this was the first person he had seen in five years, how loneliness tore at him as painfully as if it was his own claws ripping at his flesh. Then, the beast part of his brain, primitive and possessive as it was, remembered that *she* had crashed into *his* territory. Anything that found itself in his territory was his by default.

And with that, her fate was sealed.

He breathed just enough hot flame against the flight box's door to thaw the frozen jamb. He pushed until he could ease it open with his paws and snout. Squeezing through the doorway in his beast form proved impossible, and he reluctantly shifted back to his human body. His scales shimmered and disappeared, revealing human skin that was a little more sensitive to the elements.

Christ, but it's cold!

He couldn't find a blanket or anything with which to wrap around the dirigible's pilot, so he would have to be quick taking her back to his cave, where he'd left a fire roaring. He gathered her in his arms and with inhuman speed, carried her back to the place he'd called home for the last five years.

CHAPTER 2

*a*rabella was far too hot for her liking.

She pulled at her clothes, desperate for some relief to the fever that had her sweating through them. As she did so, a warm hand clamped over hers. "Don't," said an unfamiliar voice. "Your mind and body are playing tricks on you."

She tried to speak, failed, and tried again. She did the same with her eyes, but they stubbornly refused to open. All that came out was, "Mmmrrff."

"You've been out in the cold for a while," the voice said. It was male and sounded rusty, like he hadn't used it in a long time but the accent was English.

"Mmmff." As if he'd changed her tides himself, a chill slithered through her, the coldest she'd ever felt. Through chattering teeth, she managed to get out, "Where am I?"

"You crashed into the side of an Antarctic mountain." He sounded incredulous, but she couldn't tell if it was due to her stupidity at undertaking such a feat, or surviving it.

With those words, she was finally able to open her eyes. It took a moment for her vision to adjust to the darkness,

10

save for a fire burning brightly in the middle of... was she in a cave? She finally fixed her gaze on the person before her. He was a man, perhaps around her age, with tangled brown hair well past his shoulders, wearing only a pair of trousers and spectacles, both of which had seen better days. His bare chest and arms were corded with muscle, a sight that would have had Arabella blushing or intrigued in any other situation. He held a small torch in his hand, its flame glowing brightly. Before she could shrink back in fear at seeing a wild man armed with fire, he smiled, or tried to.

The gesture clearly didn't come easy to him. It quickly faded.

"Where the hell am I?" she asked, even though she already knew.

"Antarctica." He sat next to her and Arabella struggled to sit up.

It took a moment for her to rearrange the blankets and furs her body was piled with, but she was stopped from throwing them off altogether when the man put a proprietary hand over her gloved one. Even through the glove's leather and her own burning fever, she could feel his body heat, hot as his torch's flame. Her cheeks grew warm, and she pulled away.

"You were showing signs of hypothermia. You need to keep warm. I don't have the resources to perform life-saving medical procedures on you if you catch pneumonia."

Arabella left the blankets, but glared at him defiantly as she peeled off her gloves. Her hands felt sweaty against the leather. "Who are you?"

He hesitated. "Xavier Kinnon."

The name meant nothing to Arabella, but she suspected he thought she might have heard of him. "Arabella Greaves. So, Mr. Kinnon, what brought you to

Antarctica? Are you on an expedition, too? Where's your dirigible?"

He didn't answer right away. His expression shuttered. He stood up, and dusted off his dirty trousers. "Would you like something to eat or drink, Miss Greaves? I apologize for not offering earlier. My manners have deteriorated since I've been here."

It wasn't until he said the words that she realized she was thirsty. "A drink, please."

He nodded and retrieved a wineskin that had seen better days. He poured water into a fire-blackened tin cup. He heated it over the flames in his hands, with scarcely a thought about the heat. When he handed the hot cup to her, she noticed his skin was none the worse for wear after being in a fire for a few minutes.

That was definitely odd. Perhaps she was suffering from some residual hallucinations after her brush with hypothermia. She sipped it, noting its strange taste compared to the water she had aboard her dirigible. It tasted cleaner somehow, without the metallic tang preserved water usually had. "How did I get here?"

"I told you. You crashed into the side of my mountain."

Even though she'd known consciously that she was stuck in a cave following a near-death experience, his words and their impact finally hit her. "I need to get back to my dirigible," she said, and pushed aside the blankets. She rose to her feet on shaky legs. "I have to repair her balloon. I—"

"You will do no such thing during the storm."

His words were calm but didn't disguise the authoritarian note his voice had taken on. Arabella had never cared for being told what to do, and she would be damned if this strange man would tell her how she would get out of this mess now. "Mr. Kinnon, I assure you I'm perfectly capable of repairing my dirigible's balloon."

"And I assure *you*, Miss Greaves, that if you go back out there, you're going to die." Eyes the color of amber fixed on hers with an intensity she'd never seen in anyone before. "Your dirigible crashed into my mountain half a mile from here. You would quickly lose direction and likely fall victim to hypothermia again before you could reach it."

"*Your* mountain? Antarctica isn't owned by anyone…"

He interrupted her again, his voice sharper. "Anything that comes by my mountain becomes mine. I can't be much clearer about your lack of prospects of surviving out there right now. I also wouldn't be of much help if you were afflicted with frostbite and had to lose fingers or toes. I can't fix frostbite."

A chill that had nothing to do with the Antarctic storm crept down Arabella's spine.

"Do you really believe that anything that comes into contact with this mountain you've declared to be, I don't know, Mount Kinnon belongs to you?"

He blinked, and the shadow that crossed his face while he delivered his possessive statement faded away. When he spoke, his voice had returned to its original cadence. "In a manner of speaking. I apologize. It's been a long time since I've spoken to another human being."

"How long have you been here?"

He sidestepped that question. "I'll help you repair your dirigible's balloon when it's safe to do so. I have a space you can stay in until then that's more comfortable than twenty feet from a cave mouth. Follow me."

She did so, keeping a blanket to wrap around her shoulders. The material wasn't soft like she thought it would be, but almost leathery. She peered at it in the dim light offered by Mr. Kinnon's torch. Some kind of animal

13

skin? The markings stood out to her but it took a moment for her to place where they came from. With a horrified shock, she dropped the blanket, letting it drift to the dirt and stone floor. "Oh, my God!"

Mr. Kinnon turned around, torch still held aloft, a concerned expression across his face. "What is it?"

"Your blankets are made from penguins!" She had yet to see any of the birds since her crash landing, and she was horrified to think she was wearing their skins.

"Yes." He looked at her, flummoxed at her reaction.

"You can't wear penguins!" Arabella protested.

"Their skins are waterproof and the blankets are warm. Antarctica is home to several species, although if you're here to look at them, you're out of luck. They spend most of their time in the water."

"They're such sweet-looking creatures!" She thought of the pictures she had seen of the animals and how innocent they appeared.

He looked at her as if she was insane, and picked up the blanket. "Your flight costume has leather pieces, and if I'm mistaken, your boots are leather, too."

"What of it?"

"You do realize that leather comes from cows, do you not? I also didn't feel like proverbially kicking you when you were down, but your leather boots are also completely unsuited to the Antarctic." He draped the penguin blanket around her shoulders once more. "Calves are just as sweet as penguins, although I haven't met cows that stink nearly as much as the birds do. Mother cows love their babies and cry for them when they're taken away. But we still eat their meat and wear their skins. There's no difference."

He was right, which was all the more aggravating. "What about the rest of the penguin?" she asked in a small voice.

14

"I ate it. That penguin didn't die only for the sake of being a blanket." He turned away and started walking again, and Arabella caught up to him. The walls here were rougher, with deep indentations in a distinctive pattern. They looked like claw marks, like a dinosaur had once carved out this lair. He led her to a small room carved out of the rock, the walls and ceiling covered in the same claw marks as the makeshift corridor. Mr. Kinnon placed his torch in a hole that had been punched through the wall, bathing the room in firelight. He set about arranging a pile of blankets and skins that had been tossed in the corner. "It isn't fancy but you'll keep warm here. This place is the furthest away from the cave mouth, so you won't have to cope with the winds."

Arabella touched the claw marks inset in the wall. "How was this made?"

"I beg your pardon?"

Was it her imagination, or did his voice waver? "This room," she repeated. "This isn't a space that was made naturally. What kind of animal did this?"

He shrugged. "Polar bears, perhaps."

"Antarctica doesn't have polar bears. You're thinking of the Arctic," she replied.

"I'm not." He cleared his throat and looked away. "There's evidence of prehistoric bear activity in this part of the world. This cave is part of that evidence."

While Arabella wasn't a scientist and she now knew her exploration skills were lacking, she did know that there had never been any bears on the Antarctic continent. He was hiding something. Perhaps this was part of the reason he was here in the first place. "Is that how you came to arrive here? Looking for evidence of bears?" she asked.

"Among other things."

"Where's the rest of your team? Or did you do the

15

same foolish thing I did and crashed into the side of a mountain?" How the hell had he ended up here and survived?

"No."

"No to the team?"

"No, as in I don't want to discuss this right now," Mr. Kinnon replied irritably. "Are you hungry? I have plenty of dried penguin meat."

She shook her head, suppressing a shudder. "No, thank you."

"I'll let you rest. I'll wake you up in a while, because I'm not sure if you've been concussed. You'll be safe and warm here," he said.

His expression shuttered, he walked away, leaving Arabella alone by the light of the torch in the wall. Its flames flickered over the claw marks gouged into the stone, highlighting a mystery that she knew the strange Mr. Kinnon wasn't telling her about.

XAVIER WRECKED EVERYTHING he touched when it came to humans. Arabella Greaves's appearance and his subsequent actions more than proved that.

He should have left her aboard the dirigible, nursing her back to health there and sending her on her way after he repaired its balloon. Instead, he had to let himself get distracted by the first human he'd seen in five years, a pretty one at that, and he had to bring her back to his cave, his sanctuary that hadn't seen anyone but himself since he carved it out. He considered going back to her dirigible to get started on repairs. But one look outside told him that the storm was still raging and he needed to keep a close eye and ear on her, besides. He was fairly certain she wasn't

16

concussed but his medical knowledge was limited, largely to his own unique physiology.

So, he returned to his own carved-out bedroom, larger than the space he allotted Miss Greaves. A penguin skin was stretched out across its doorway, allowing him some privacy, and he easily breathed across the torches he kept along the wall to light them. His bedroom was exactly as he left it. His human relics from his days before he took up residence in an Antarctic mountain were neatly arranged next to his makeshift bed draped with penguin skins. His little-worn clothes were left in a neatly folded pile in the corner, along with a small stack of books and a journal that he long ago filled.

He hadn't written in years. Once an avid diarist, he'd given it up shortly after he arrived. There was nothing new left to observe about himself at this point, nor was there anything left to observe of the penguins, his only companions. They could scarcely be called companions when one had to eat them. Xavier supposed he would never stop feeling guilty about that.

He wondered if Miss Greaves had any edible food left aboard her dirigible, if she would mind if he pilfered some. He was desperate for a cup of tea or coffee after so many years.

Perhaps she would leave her stash behind when she left Antarctica. She *would* leave. He would personally ensure that even though a part of him wanted to keep her with him. Humans were too delicate for the harsh climate, and he already knew this particular human was too delicate for him.

Too delicate for me. As if she was a plaything instead of a person. He mentally shook himself for thinking of her in such a way. His inner dragon seemed to agree with that Neanderthal thought. It urged him to shift, to show itself to Miss Greaves and see her reaction. If Xavier didn't know any better, he would have thought it was trying to fulfill a role, a fantasy built about the mythos of a dragon spiriting away a princess.

"Miss Greaves isn't a princess," he murmured aloud. "Just a very foolish traveler with too much money and time on her hands." And money she came from. Even in his mad dash to rescue her when he'd been in his dragon form, he recognized her dirigible's superior craftsmanship and custom fittings. Her flight clothes were high quality and very expensive.

His dragon growled, a noise that escaped Xavier's throat. Since he had no intention of showing himself in his dragon form to the sleeping woman in his spare room, he had to leave his cave to let the beast out, to stretch its wings. *Blast it, I've already been outside today.* While he was better equipped for the cold than most, it was still inconceivably freezing outside and he didn't relish exposing himself to it. But it was better than facing Arabella Greaves in his dragon form. So, with a sigh, he walked to the front of the cave and pushed aside its penguin hide door to step out, snowflakes immediately hitting him in the face with the help of gusting winds. Xavier stripped out of his trousers and let his beast overtake him, his body shifting and elongating, scales popping up along his skin. With a roar of delight, he sailed into the air on green scaled wings.

CHAPTER 3

*torch's flames burned low from the crudely carved out sconce on the wall, a focal point for Arabella as she stirred. She always knew where she was upon waking; she never came to bleary and confused. The sole exception was coming to in the same cave she found herself in, and she dejectedly realized that nothing about this Antarctic nightmare had been a dream.

What time is it? She didn't have her watch on her, and she supposed it was back at the dirigible.

Perhaps Mr. Kinnon would know. She rose from her pallet of penguin skins—*ugh*—on wobbling legs and took a few short, halting steps out of her room, noting again the claw-like marks on the walls. What in God's name made those? She didn't believe it was a prehistoric bear for a second. She took the torch from the wall and held it aloft, its dying embers offering little in the way of light. Keeping her free hand on the scarred rock wall, Arabella felt her way along the corridor to the cave's main area. "Mr. Kinnon?" She poked her head into the other room she'd noticed, its doorway draped with another penguin skin, ubiquitous in this strange place. "Mr. Kinnon?"

It was clearly a personal space. A small stack of neatly folded clothes and a few books and leather-bound journals were arranged next to a bed made up of penguin skins. But Xavier Kinnon was nowhere to be found.

Had he up and left her to her own devices?

Perhaps he'd gone out to fetch more penguins for food, she reasoned. The thought sent a measure of relief through her. Mr. Kinnon had been living here for years on his own and was unlikely to abandon his home just because she had the misfortune of crashing into his mountain.

Bracing herself against the cold, she pulled back the penguin skin curtain door at the mouth of the cave. Just inside it was a pair of men's trousers, not unlike the ones her rescuer wore earlier, a set of spectacles on top.

If his trousers were here, where was he?

Panic gripped her. "Mr. Kinnon?" she shouted into the wind. She thought the storm might have died down since she was asleep, but she couldn't be sure. Wrapping her blanket around herself a little more tightly, she ventured further from the cave mouth. Antarctica's perpetual early evening darkness greeted her. Arabella's vision was impeded by swirling snow. "Mr. Kinnon?" Her words were swallowed by the wind and she inhaled a few snowflakes.

An otherworldly cry from above had her looking upward in fright.

It took a few seconds for her to recognize the cause of the noise, and even then, she didn't believe her eyes.

Scales.

Deep green scales flecked with black and gold spots appeared a scant few feet above her head. She was so preoccupied with the sight of the scales that she didn't recognize the shape they formed, the gigantic otherworldly being gliding on the wind above her. Fire issued from its mouth as it cried out again, the flames swallowed by the storm.

Arabella was in the presence of an honest-to-God dragon.

Her first thought was she had contracted altitude sickness and was hallucinating. She had no idea how high up she was on Mr. Kinnon's mountain, but it was certainly higher than anywhere she'd ever been that wasn't in the air. That had to be it. There was no way she could possibly be looking upon a dragon. She couldn't tear her eyes away from the gigantic, fire-breathing lizard above her as he circled around the mountain. His magnificent blue-green wings shimmered, almost glowing.

Big golden eyes caught hers.

She could've sworn she saw the dragon flinch in a very human way. His flight slowed and he came to a graceful landing in the snow, his clawed feet hardly reacting to the cold contact.

Arabella remained rooted to the spot, mesmerized. "Altitude sickness," she murmured to herself. Or hypothermia. The wind whipped cruelly through her clothes. Her coat was no match for the Antarctic chill, and as the dragon slowly walked toward her, the realization that she was about to die hit her with an unexpected, uncanny calm. "I never left the dirigible," she whispered. The puffs her breath left in the air were stolen by the wind. "I'm still there. I'm going to freeze to death in a few seconds." She couldn't force herself to move. The dragon snorted and released a thin trail of smoke through his nostrils. As Arabella watched, his form shrank and glowed, shifting into the shape of a naked man, barefoot.

She blinked until Mr. Kinnon's face came into focus.

The last thing she remembered before she fainted dead

away was his shouting, "What the everloving hell are you doing out here?"

~

FOR THE SECOND time in as many days, Xavier carried Miss Greaves back into his cave. He stoked the fire near its mouth, reviving its flames. He draped a penguin skin over her, then put on his trousers. He sat in front of the fire, next to her, and waited.

This time, she didn't stay unconscious for that long. Her dark lashes fluttered against her pale cheeks. "Damn," she said, and sat up, clutching the skin to her.

She hadn't run off screaming about dragons, but he still waited for the inevitable panic about seeing him in his beast form. He was angry with himself for not being more careful and leaving the mountain's vicinity for his flight. He'd worried she'd taken it upon herself to repair her dirigible or start searching for him.

"Altitude sickness," she said.

"I beg your pardon?"

"Altitude sickness," she repeated. "I think I have it. How else could one explain why I saw a dragon outside?"

Indecision warred within Xavier. He didn't want her to think she was ill when she wasn't, but he wasn't prepared to give up his secrets, either. He reminded himself that she was returning to England, or at least getting the hell away from Antarctica, as soon as possible. It wasn't as if anyone would believe she had spotted a dragon there, anyway.

"He turned into you," she continued. She squinted at him, blue eyes fixing on his face.

He fought the urge to squirm in place, a sure admission of guilt.

"Are hallucinations a symptom of altitude sickness?" she asked.

He shrugged his shoulders noncommittally. "I don't know. I've been here so long that I don't experience those symptoms."

"Where's your shirt?"

"I'm not that bothered by the cold anymore."

"It has to be a hundred degrees below zero!"

"One can get used to anything if one is exposed to it long enough," Xavier said.

"I saw your trousers by the door. I saw you turn into…" She tilted her head, and he thought about his nude form when he shifted. She was undoubtedly thinking about that, too. "I saw you turn into you," she finished.

"Perhaps you've discovered a new symptom of altitude sickness, one unique to the Antarctic continent," he said. Trying to change the conversation's direction, he asked, "You wouldn't happen to have any coffee or tea aboard your dirigible, would you?"

She didn't answer his question. "I could've sworn you were a dragon."

"Dragons don't exist," he replied automatically. His voice was steadier than he thought it would be when lying. He hadn't had anyone to lie to in years and he thought he might be out of practice. Instead of arguing, she surprised him when she walked straight up to him, so close he could feel her body heat radiating off her. He thought he could detect the faintest aroma of her soap, something expensive and imported from outside England. She surprised him again when she leaned to his neck and sniffed his bare skin. Every sense went into overdrive, every hair on his body standing at attention at the small gesture. An unexpected and unwelcome flash of arousal zinged through his body.

He quickly stepped away before his body's reactions became more obvious. "What the devil was that for?"

"You smell like smoke."

"Of course I would smell like smoke." He thumbed in the direction of the fire, still burning cheerfully near the cave's mouth.

"Not just smoke. You smell a little like sulfur," she said.

Mortification bloomed in him, bright as the sun that he seldom saw. His male pride was wounded for the first time in... he couldn't remember how long. *I smell like sulfur?* He raised his forearm and sniffed it. *My God, I do smell like sulfur.* Why not of the outdoors, of the crispy snow that would blanket the outside of his mountain kingdom when the storm let up? Or even of the earthy smell of the mountain he'd carved his home out of? Anything but the scent of hell. He stiffened and moved further away from her. "I don't smell of sulfur," he retorted. "And it appears that your injuries are worse than I previously thought if you're having hallucinations. Do you have any medicine aboard your dirigible?"

"You just asked about coffee and tea."

"I can't ask about medicine, either?"

Irritation laced her words. "I have some plasters and Dr. Thaddeus's Miracle Elixir in my dirigible."

"What the hell is a miracle elixir?" Before she could reply, he said, "Never mind. I see quack patent medicines are still the rage in England."

"It is not a quack medicine. I purchased it from an apothecary in Knightsbridge."

"It's certainly a quack medicine in that case but I'll go fetch it if you think it will help with your Antarctic sickness. That's what I've decided to call your condition."

"I'm not unwell, other than the symptoms one can expect from a dirigible crash."

"Which can include head injuries." Xavier was tired of this conversation. "And do you have any coffee or..."

"Yes," she said shortly. "I have several boxes of tea. Please help yourself."

Xavier nodded. "I'll be back." He turned away from her, walking around the firepit to the cave's entrance.

"Wait," she said.

He paused, heart thundering in his chest. What was she going to bring up now?

"Aren't you going to put on a coat? Or at least a shirt?"

Xavier gritted his teeth. Frustration at his own carelessness welled up inside him. "Of course," he said. Without another word, he strode to his room. He pulled on his last intact shirt and his coat. He slung the strap of his old satchel from his university days over his shoulder before leaving the cave and a suspicious-looking Miss Greaves.

CHAPTER 4

*A*rabella had to fight with a primitive part of herself that wanted to take in a shirtless Xavier Kinnon in all his bare-skinned glory, and she was proud of winning that battle. Now that he was gone, disappeared into the swirling snow in little more than a shirt and trousers, she had ample time to ruminate on what he termed her hallucinations.

She hadn't imagined anything she'd seen earlier. She knew, in her heart, that she saw a dragon soaring above her and that dragon had shifted into the Englishman who took her into his rough-hewn mountain home. She'd seen him naked, impervious to the cold, and Mr. Kinnon had nearly marched out into the snowstorm without a coat before she reminded him of it. That kind of tolerance to the Antarctic chill wasn't possible for humans.

Perhaps he was in his dragon form again. Now that she felt like she was mostly back to normal, she could venture out of the cave and see him shifted for herself. A small voice in the back of her mind warned her that it might be a mistake, yet another in a series of them that led her to be

26

stranded on this mountain. Arabella could handle the cold in short doses. She wouldn't venture too far from the cave. She would just take a peek outside and see if a dragon flew overhead. Her decision made, she slipped on her heavy coat and stuck her hands in her lined leather gloves before venturing out of the cave. Wind whipped at her face, sending tiny, icy needles into her skin, and she adjusted her scarf to better protect her face. The sky was darker than she expected and she looked back at the cave mouth, wondering if she should turn around.

Nonsense. I'm hardly leaving the area.

She wandered a few feet, head upturned to the dark sky, looking for... what? A flash of scales overhead? A jet of fire? When the sensation of cold stinging needles against her exposed forehead became too much, she turned her vision to the ground at the footprints in the snow. They were already filling in. "Damn," she murmured behind her scarf. "I should have looked down first." She hoped she didn't lose her way as she followed the footprints wherever they led. They disappeared after a while. Whether they were filled in from the snow or Xavier had taken off into the sky, Arabella couldn't tell. She turned around and started to make her way back to the cave, following her own footprints back.

They too vanished after a few feet.

"How is it this dark?" she said aloud, her voice carried away by the wind. "It's supposed to be summer." Just as quickly, she remembered the New York airfield comptroller informing her that it wasn't summer in the southern hemisphere. There wasn't so much as a sliver of moonlight to guide her by, let alone stars. Tears threatened to fill her eyes but she willed them away, terrified of freezing her eyes closed. She was, as her father would have put it, a weapons-grade imbecile. She was lost and disoriented, trapped in an uninhabited land with a dragon man and unable to leave.

I'm going to die here.

The realization clogged her throat with a cry of frustration and grief that begged to be released. She would die for what? Just to prove to others that she could travel to Antarctica? It wasn't as if Antarctica was at all interesting aside from penguins and their guano. She wasn't even here for the penguins and hadn't considered them until Mr. Kinnon gave her that blanket. A sob escaped her and she willed away her tears again, and she did the only thing she could think of doing to save herself. Her scream was nearly swallowed by the wind, but she dearly hoped dragon men had sensitive hearing and could hear her panicked "Mr. Kinnon!" across the frozen landscape.

An odd vibration sounded through Xavier's head, traveling down his body and freezing him in place for a moment. He nearly dropped the tin of tea leaves he held as he tried to figure out what the hell had just happened. He felt it again, but this time his ears picked up his name, and there was only one person in the whole of Antarctica who would be doing that. "What the devil has she got herself into now?" he grumbled. He looked around the dirigible's cabin for his clothes, then remembered that he left them in the enclosed deck above him. Sighing in irritation, he hauled himself up a ladder to the deck.

"*Mr. Kinnon!*"

Xavier heard her more clearly now, her fright tangible. "Damn," he muttered as he quickly slipped on his clothing and boots. He slung his old leather satchel over his shoulder, the bag now packed with Miss Greaves's entire stash of tea and Dr. Thaddeus's Miracle Elixir that she claimed worked for all sorts of maladies. As he put on his coat, the scent of sulfur wafted to his nostrils and he sighed. He really did smell like a dragon. At least he'd pilfered one of her paper-wrapped bars of soap for his own use. As he hurried through the snow, he frantically sniffed the air for Miss Greaves's scent. He contemplated telling his uninvited guest the truth. Or confirming it, since she already knew.

He hadn't spoken to another human for five years. He hadn't realized until he set foot aboard her dirigible that he missed conversation so much, even if the other person was a reckless fool who traveled to Antarctica alone during the winter. He could parse out her scent, but it was difficult to pinpoint in his human form, mingled as it was with the constant smell of fresh snow and beneath that, penguin shit. He could tell she had wandered a significant distance from the cave and that she was in grave danger.

He sighed.

If he dallied around any longer, she was going to collapse, or worse, in the cold darkness. The easiest way to find her would be to shift. "Damn it," he muttered again. He stripped once more and shoved his clothes into his satchel. His boots stuck out at odd angles from the bag. He scarcely felt the cold beneath his bare feet as he concentrated. He tried to push away his irritation that Miss Greaves had ignored his instructions again as his body shifted. Taking care to pick up his precious bag of tea with his claws, he let the wind lift him into the air and he hovered. His vision scanned the wintry landscape for an idiot in fashionably inappropriate flight gear.

He found her easily enough, and was surprised to see that she'd wandered about a quarter of a mile away from their cave. She must have turned herself around a time or two, because she was in the opposite direction of where her dirigible crashed. *His* cave, he mentally corrected himself. His wings beat the air, disturbing the pattern of snow falling nearly sideways. It was *his* lair, with *his* treasures, and he had carved it out himself to hide his hoard deep in the mountain. He pushed his possessiveness aside and focused on Miss Greaves. He gave a breathy dragon sigh, a motion that had some fire leaving his mouth.

She looked up, her eyes wide as saucers.

That was all he could see, since she had wrapped up the rest of her face in a scarf, which must have been the most practical thing she had done since she took off from London alone. If he had confirmed her suspicions in the first place, had acknowledged that her eyes weren't deceiving her when he flew around his mountain earlier, she wouldn't be wandering around in an Antarctic blizzard right now. He came to a graceful landing a few yards away from her. His vision, green-tinged when he was in his dragon form, could still make out the shocked look in her eyes.

"Mr. Kinnon!" she exclaimed from behind her scarf.

Xavier cleared his throat, releasing more flames.

She jumped back a few inches, even though she was nowhere near his mouth.

After a couple of tries, he managed to say, "My back." The words came out in a growl.

Miss Greaves straightened. She took a few cautious steps toward him. "I beg your pardon?"

This is what she says when a dragon speaks to her? 'I beg your pardon'? Xavier tamped down his irritation and tried again. "Get on my back." Smoke issued from his nostrils, and he had to speak quietly to prevent himself from breathing fire accidentally. "I'll take us home." It was *his* home, and *his* hoard he was guarding, but it was easier to say "home" instead of "my mountain" when in this form.

But she shook her head. "How do I know you won't drop me?"

His incredulity grew. They were in a potentially life or death situation, with death far more certain for her. She was worried that he would drop her? He thought about shifting back to his human form and guiding her back to the cave, but decided not to. For one, it would be faster to fly back, and second, he didn't want to deal with her being scandalized over seeing a naked man in the snow again. He could also see that despite her bravado, she was freezing. He would be surprised if none of her fingers or toes had frostbite at this point. "Don't argue," he said through gritted teeth.

Miss Greaves didn't move for a moment and simply stared at him.

Xavier stared back, hoping he didn't look too frightening.

"All right," she finally agreed, closing the short distance between them.

Xavier pressed his belly to the ground to give her better purchase for climbing. He couldn't keep from yelping a little when she stepped on the bony part of his wing..

"I'm sorry," she said, and wiggled further up his back. She wrapped her arms around his neck, so tightly that it hurt a little to swallow.

Xavier's scales weren't terribly sensitive to heat or cold, but he could feel her human warmth better than he expected he would, even through her layers of clothes. It was more acute than the blizzard raging around them and lit an odd warmth inside him that had nothing to do with his fire-breathing capabilities when he was in this form. It felt good and he didn't like that, not in the least because she was so reckless.

Speaking of reckless... His claws tightened around his

31

satchel. It wouldn't do to drop it and the precious caffeine it contained. *And one of my last sets of clothes.* They were threadbare and he had haphazardly repaired them countless times since his arrival in Antarctica. He couldn't afford to lose them while he still had a guest.

He glided to a stop outside the cave mouth, its penguin hide door gently flapping in the wind. Miss Greaves hadn't thought to secure it with the rocks he dug out for such a purpose. He sighed, accidentally releasing some fire. She shrieked from her spot on his back. She could scarcely slide off him fast enough, and her bootheel hit the sensitive part of his wing again.

Instead of ducking under the curtain for the cave's relative warmth, she waited, arms crossed over her chest.

He resisted the urge to sigh again, knowing she wanted to see him shift and hear his explanation. No one had ever seen him shift until she arrived. He tried not to feel awkward as he dropped his satchel into the snow. He stood up to his full height when he finished shifting and picked up the satchel. His gaze met Miss Greaves's, her expression unreadable in her eyes. "Fancy some tea?" he asked, and strode into the cave without waiting for an answer.

CHAPTER 5

The fire had all but gone out. Arabella silently cursed her own earlier carelessness when she didn't secure the penguin skin curtain in place before she rushed out after Mr. Kinnon. She silently stoked the embers, coaxing them back to life, before she unwound her scarf from around her face.

He faced her, naked as the day he was born, after he fixed the curtain back in place. Unsure where she should look, Arabella stared at the fire.

"Can you breathe on it when it goes out?" she asked.

"Miss Greaves," he began, but faltered.

Arabella forged on. "You don't have to call me that. Arabella is fine. No one worth mentioning in England has ever called me Miss Greaves."

He was quiet as he wrapped a penguin skin around his midsection, likely for her benefit. He unpacked his satchel, filled with his clothes and tins from her dirigible's stores. She noticed he brought her bottle of Dr. Thaddeus's Miracle Elixir, and she was touched that he remembered it. "I hope you understand my situation," he finally said.

33

"That you're a dragon and you lied to me about it? How long did you think you could keep that a secret? We're the only two people between here and Santiago!"

He inspected a tea tin and lifted its lid, inhaling deeply over it. He wore an expression that could only be described as blissful, the only time Arabella had ever seen anything happy there. It was a marked change in appearance for him.

He should do that more often. She gave her head a little shake to remind herself about the impossible subject at hand. "How are you a dragon, anyway?"

He shrugged his bare shoulders, and his usual cautious look returned. "I suppose it came from one or both of my parents."

"They didn't tell you?"

"They died when I was four years old," he replied shortly. "Twenty-seven years ago. I hardly remember them. Anyway, I don't know any other dragons to ask. Do you suppose it's too late for tea?"

"I don't know what time it is. It's always near dark or full dark here."

"I can check my pocket watch for certain, but it's around five in the evening. Hell, I believe I'll boil some water. I haven't had a cup of tea in years." He started to rise to his feet, but Arabella stopped him with a motion of her hand.

She retrieved the dented metal bucket full of half-melted snow that he kept near the door and hauled it to the fire pit, along with the rough-hewn bowl carved by claws that held his dried penguin meat. "You never told me if you can breathe on the fire to keep it going. I don't imagine there are a great deal of trees from which to make firewood." She took out a strip of meat, sighed, and ate it, trying not think about where it came from. It was too fatty and fishy-tasting for her liking.

"There aren't any trees here," he confirmed. "To answer your question, yes, I can breathe fire when I want to." He poured a small measure of tea leaves into a metal cup, then gently poured some water from the bucket over it. He held it over the fire, which had grown to a more respectable size.

"You won't burn yourself?"

"No."

"I have a teapot on my dirigible," she said.

"I'll retrieve that next." The skin on his hand rippled and shifted, and Arabella blinked, unsure if her eyes were playing tricks on her.

Fascinated, she watched as a few scales formed on his arm and his hand extended into claws over the flames. She couldn't keep herself from asking, "You can partially change? How did you do that?" Too late, she wondered if it was a rude question.

"I learned how to do it when I came here," he replied.

"Is that why *you* came here?"

He gave the barest of nods, gaze not meeting hers, and held his hand over the fire until the water in his cup boiled.

"Perhaps we could go back to my dirigible for the teapot," she said again, watching as he inhaled the tea's steam.

"Later," he replied. "I don't feel like chasing you across the snow again."

"I wouldn't have done that if you told me the truth to begin with," Arabella protested. A horrible, terrifying thought struck her. Would Mr. Kinnon ever let her leave, now that he knew she knew what he was? Would he keep her alive? She swallowed, a whole new wave of fear crashing into her.

He must have picked up on it, because his blissful expression disappeared. He clutched his cup, his knuckles turning white. "What is it?"

How did one bring up one's potential murder? "Um," she said uselessly.

His gaze probed her, and she didn't detect a hint of malice there. "Arabella? What's troubling you?"

She hated that her stomach did a strange little flutter that had nothing to do with fear when he used her first name. She lifted an eyebrow, and a sheepish expression crossed his face.

"Besides being stranded in Antarctica," he added.

"What are you going to do with me?" she blurted. Her next words tumbled out, an edge of panic to them that she couldn't help. "Will you let me leave? *Can* I even leave this place?"

He froze in place and didn't reply for a moment. When he did, his voice was preternaturally calm. "I won't force you to stay against your will. I would never do that to anyone. I'll help you be on your way home when it's safe to repair your dirigible. I only ask that you not tell anyone I'm here."

"You're not going to kill me?"

His features contorted in horror, then indignation. "Of course not." He stiffened. "I'm insulted you would ask. If I wanted you dead, I would have left you in your dirigible or out in the snow this evening." His expression hardened and his grip on his cup tightened. "That was a monumentally stupid thing to do."

"I suppose it was just one more monumentally stupid thing I've done recently."

"Of course." Mr. Kinnon relaxed a little when she agreed with him. "If you're going to leave this place alive, you have to listen to me when I say to stay in place.

36

This isn't an area known for its hospitality toward humans."

Suitably chastised, Arabella reached for the bottle of Dr. Thaddeus's Miracle Elixir. She tried to remove the cap but quickly realized it was frozen shut. "Damn," she muttered, and set the patent medicine closer to the fire to thaw out.

He reached for it. "What is this, anyway?"

"It helps with common ailments."

He sniffed at it. "Can you buy it in the shops without a prescription?"

She nodded. "Yes."

"I can smell sugar in this," he reported, and set down the bottle. "It's nothing more than a placebo."

Irritation welled up in her and she snatched the bottle away. The cold glass was almost comforting, a reminder of her life in the skies. "It helps with headaches and general malaise."

"It does not. It doesn't have any laudanum in it, which would have made it effective. Unfortunately, laudanum also has undesirable and often fatal effects."

The reason Arabella liked the elixir so much was because it was devoid of laudanum. Her stomach clenched at the mere mention of the word. "I know it doesn't," she said evenly. "I go out of my way to avoid it."

"A wise decision."

It was, but Arabella hadn't made it for the reasons he might have suspected. It had nothing to do with research and everything to do with the impact laudanum had on her family. The memory of her mother hit her with all the force of the winds outside the cave. In that moment, she missed her fiercely. "Yes," she said curtly. She rose to her feet, the bottle in her hand. "My mother died from an overdose of it nearly twenty years ago, courtesy of a physician's recommendation. If you'll excuse me, I believe I'll return to my room."

She didn't wait for a response before leaving.

THE DEPTHS of Xavier's own stupidity could still surprise him. Stupidity, and insensitivity.

Had Arabella been foolish? Of course.

Could he have handled things better? Absolutely.

She'd been here only a couple of days, not nearly long enough to truly understand the dangers Antarctica posed. He suspected she did now, and he wished he could have emphasized them a little more respectfully.

It wasn't just the Antarctic dangers. He'd needlessly insulted her over the harmless patent medicine she took for whatever purposes *and* dredged up memories of her late mother in the process. It was nothing more than sugar water dyed with beet juice, far more harmless than the scads of other patent medicines cramming apothecary shelves across England. However, it provided a measure of comfort for her during a stressful time, and he spoiled it for her.

Just like he spoiled everything for everyone.

He needed to apologize. He swallowed the last of his tea and stood up, the penguin skin blanket falling away.

I should probably dress first.

He quickly put on the clothes he'd stuffed in his satchel, and barefoot, made his way to Arabella's room.

She sat on the floor, knees drawn to her chest. She looked up at Xavier standing in the doorway. "Hello."

Awkwardness descended over him. "I came to apologize."

"For what?"

38

"Not being kinder to you," he replied. "I can list everything I've done wrong since you crashed here, if you like."

That remark drew a small smile from her. "You've been right all along about my monumental stupidity."

"I could have worded that better. I also apologize for the insults. Your medicine is important to you, and if you think it works, there's no harm in it." He paused, considering his next words. "I'm sorry for bringing up your mother's passing, too."

"You didn't. I did that. You had no way of knowing that she was given far too much cough medicine for a simple cold." She quickly changed the subject. "I didn't think lizards had such a thorough sense of smell to pick up scent from a stoppered bottle."

That pricked at his pride. "I'm not a lizard."

"Aren't dragons related to them?"

His lack of clear knowledge about that potential connection also rankled him. "I don't know. Possibly. How do you know about lizards' lack of smell?"

"Books and zoos." She relaxed a little, unwinding her arms from around her knees. She straightened out her legs on the rough-hewn floor. "I'm an explorer, Mr. Kinnon. I'm motivated by curiosity."

"Xavier," he said, the response immediate.

"I beg your pardon?"

"Just call me Xavier. We're the only two people in this godforsaken place." Hesitating for a moment, unsure how the gesture would be received, he sat next to her, back against the wall. He could feel the marks his own claws made when he carved out this space against his skin. It was a reminder of what he was, how he didn't belong in Arabella's world. She didn't move away. A small part of him rejoiced at that.

"Xavier," she said, her voice a little cautious, like she was testing out his name.

It was the first time in five years that anyone had called him that. Maybe longer, since the research crew he traveled with called him "Mr. Kinnon" or "Dr. Kinnon." He hadn't realized how much he missed that small connection with someone. "Yes?"

"Will you come back to England with me?"

He hadn't expected that question. "Absolutely not." It was an automatic response.

"Why?"

He fought the urge to point out the obvious as rudely as possible. "I can't go back like this."

"You can't be the only dragon out there," she insisted. "There must be others."

"There are other shifters," he bit out. "But no dragons and those shifters are to be left as they are, by order of the government." Arabella didn't speak for a few seconds, and he wondered if he'd actually managed to shock her into silence. Or issued a death sentence to her. The existence of shapeshifters was a state secret. "Please forget I said anything about shifters."

"Oh, no." Arabella faced him, one eyebrow arched. "I won't say anything, because everyone will think I'm mad, but you're not going to casually mention the existence of shapeshifters under government watch and then expect me to forget about them."

"I've said too much."

"You haven't said enough."

"I've only heard rumors," he explained. "I've found some corroborating evidence of a pack's existence in the north, but I would never contact them. They aren't supposed to be dragons, besides."

To his surprise, she didn't needle him for more information about the werewolf pack he suspected to be somewhere in Scotland. Instead, she asked, "Do you think it's possible that mermaids are real?"

"I'm sure there are any number of supernatural creatures among us. As long as they keep to themselves, I say they should be left alone. That's what I'm doing here. Keeping to myself." Addressing her question directly, he added, "Do you think you encountered a mermaid at one point?"

"Not me. My family owns a property in a miserable village on the seaside. I never go there if I can help it. We rented it to a writer last year and there was an accident with its underwater ballroom, and…"

Xavier couldn't help himself. "Why the devil would it have an underwater ballroom?"

"See, I've asked myself and my family that exact question over the years. It was an accident waiting to happen, and it did when that writer moved in. A substantial part of the house was destroyed. He and his, well, lady friend I suppose, survived it, but the property's caretaker didn't." A shadow crossed her face. "His widow said he was convinced the writer's friend was a mermaid. It was a bizarre story, and the village itself is quite superstitious and strange. I thought it was the rambling of a grieving widow, but now that I've met you, I'm not so sure."

Unexpected hope flared in him at her words, at the possibility of her connection, no matter how tenuous, to another shifter. "Where are they now?"

"I haven't the foggiest. I wrote to them when they returned to London and I received a reply that mentioned they were traveling around Britain for a while. Of course, I wouldn't rely on the inhabitants of Gull's End to be truthful, or at least not superstitious." She paused. "Although after meeting you, they may have been on to something regarding that writer's friend being a mermaid."

Disappointment replaced Xavier's fleeting happiness. "There must be a way to find them."

She shrugged. "That would involve you leaving Antarctica."

She had him there. "I suppose so. If I ever left, I would seek out the wolves in Scotland, anyway. I have to know if they actually exist."

"Assuming they don't tear you limb from limb after hunting them down," she pointed out.

"You truly are a barrel of sunshine, aren't you?" The words escaped Xavier's mouth before he could reconsider their potential impact. "I would be arriving peacefully," he emphasized. "I also have my own means of defense should they get aggressive, and I'll respect their decision if they tell me to leave their territory. I'm not a threat to them at all. Wolves are pack animals. Dragons aren't, as far as I can tell."

"There must be others like you," Arabella insisted again.

"If there are, they want nothing to do with me," he replied bitterly. The conversation had taken a turn he didn't care for, and he regretted not leaving her be after he apologized for his earlier behavior. He rose to his feet. "I should let you get some rest. You've had quite a day."

She narrowed her eyes at him, a defiant look that did something to his insides.

It was a sensation he hadn't felt in years. The pull of a good debate, someone who wasn't afraid to stand up to him. In his old life, those qualities in a woman never failed to capture his attention. What a shame that he felt those stirrings for someone whose stubbornness was rooted in stupid decisions.

"On the contrary," Arabella said. Now it was her turn to stand up, and he noticed for the first time that she was nearly as tall as he was. "I would like to talk about this further."

He closed his eyes, forcing himself not to snap at her. Breathed deeply, and thought he caught the faint scent of that alleged miracle elixir and her soap. *God damn it all. That smells good.* He opened his eyes and fixed his gaze on hers. "If we are to cohabitate in my mountain, we must respect one another's boundaries. I don't wish to continue this conversation. Would you want to discuss painful topics? Rejection, perhaps?"

Something in her expression shuttered, and he knew he'd struck something raw in her. Her jaw ticked. "Understood," she said stiffly. "Leave me, then." Arabella leaned against the wall and slid back down to the rough-hewn floor.

The entire room was marred with marks of his claws. Xavier still remembered the feeling of stone ripping away under them as he furiously ripped out a place to call his own all those years ago. He'd shocked himself at his own strength.

He was too dangerous to be around humans.

He nodded at Arabella, now sitting again with her knees drawn up to her chest. "Very well," he replied, and left the room.

CHAPTER 6

*S*he couldn't stay here.

A curious mixture of rage, frustration, and homesickness welled in Arabella as she considered her predicament. She needed to leave Antarctica as soon as she could, forget she had ever taken this foolhardy journey. She could return to Santiago, recover for a few days and perhaps take in some sightseeing, before setting back for...

Where? Where should I go next?

She had no permanent home other than the dirigible and she preferred not to spend time at the house her father shared with his new wife. Clarinda was mortified by Arabella's existence, by her nomadic lifestyle, and had made it clear she wasn't willing to respect her so long as she lived among the clouds.

Arabella rued the day Clarinda civilized her father, and all but turned him against her.

She wasn't sure how much time had passed, but after what felt like hours, she was tired of stewing by herself. She left her makeshift bed of penguin skins to find Xavier. He wasn't in the carved-out space he used as his room. The

44

cave mouth door was undisturbed, and she didn't dare try to venture outside again to look for him.

Where the hell could he be?

She looked at the corridor a few yards away from his room and sighed. He was likely in wherever that led to. He hadn't shown her that area on his tour when he rescued her, but he hadn't explicitly told her to avoid it, either. It was a dark tunnel, scarcely wide enough for her to fit through, with a faint glow visible from somewhere inside.

Was heading in there another stupid decision?

Possibly, she thought, but she was still going to see where he spent his time when he wasn't in his house. Bracing her hands on either side of the walls, she began a slow, careful walk through the corridor. The indentations caused by his claws reminded her of his power, and she hoped her checking out the space wouldn't be received too badly. It took a few moments for her brain to register that she was descending a makeshift set of stairs. The air felt like it changed, tasted different, as she walked further into the mountain. She kept her eyes on the light, a beacon in the strange darkness. "Xavier?" she called.

Was it her imagination, or did she hear an animalistic snort?

She tried again. "Xavier, are you down here?" The light grew brighter, and she reached a landing where a lone torch glowed from a clawed-out wall sconce. It looked like there was another set of stairs to descend, and Arabella peered down them.

The light bounced off green dragon scales, and a gigantic head was raised. Xavier's dragon eyes pierced hers, the expression inscrutable.

Arabella raised her hands in a show of surrender. "Can I come down and visit?"

45

He cocked his head to the side, then raised a clawed foot, gesturing toward himself.

Arabella took that as a yes and carefully climbed down the stairs, holding the wall for purchase. "I've really bungled this, haven't I? Even more than I thought possible for a botched Antarctic expedition."

He made a snuffling sound that she couldn't decipher.

She looked around the dim space, noting the glittery stalactites that dangled from the ceiling, pointy and lethal. "Are those diamonds?"

He made another noise, this one from his throat, that she took as another affirmative.

"Xavier, is this where you keep treasure?" Her tins of tea were stacked in a neat pile near his tail. She picked one up and inspected it. "Is this your newest acquisition?" Suddenly, she understood. This was his lair. He had given in to his dragon impulses, the ones she read about in storybooks as a child and hidden himself away with his treasure, meager as it was. "I had no idea diamonds could be found in Antarctica." A cluster of glittering rocks called to her from the wall, and she reached out a hand to touch them, fascinated.

Xavier's reaction was swift. His tail grabbed her around the waist and pulled her away from the wall, holding her against him. A growl issued from his throat.

She couldn't help herself. Her scream bounced off the walls, but he didn't let her go. "I'm sorry!" She fought against him, hands grappling with his scales, cool to the touch. "I won't touch your things. You can keep my tea!" She wiggled against him, but he didn't release his hold on her. "Xavier, let me go!"

He swung her around with a terrifying speed and strength until she could see his face.

"Xavier," she repeated. She damned the waver in her

voice. "I'm not going to touch your diamonds. Let me go." She was let go so quickly she nearly fell to the floor.

Xavier quickly shifted into his human form and stood on unsteady legs, a mixture of panic and shame across his face in the flickering torchlight. He stared at her, unable to speak. He opened his mouth, thought better of what he was going to say, and closed it.

Arabella wasn't sure how to respond, either. Finally, she pointed out the obvious. "I shouldn't have come down here."

He looked away and shrugged, but the motion did nothing to smooth away the tension Arabella could see in his body. "You would've come exploring sooner or later."

"I'm sure I breached some form of etiquette. That wouldn't be the first for me."

"Me, neither," Xavier replied, voice soft. "I apologize. I wasn't thinking. It was an automatic reaction. This is my hoard." He raised a hand, as if to indicate the glittering ceiling and walls.

"And my tea," Arabella said.

"Potentially your entire dirigible if I lost my mind and sunk my claws into it. I like to collect things."

"Is that why you came here?"

He nodded. "It was a big reason. I can't go destroying villages and stealing treasures when I'm thousands of miles away from humans." Turning away from her, he slipped a loose, hand-sewn shirt over his head, followed by trousers with a drawstring waist.

"Tea is treasure?"

"It is when you haven't had a cup in five years. As are all the other odds and ends on your dirigible." He paused. "And you."

His words hit her with all the impact of a steam cab at full speed down a London street. "I beg your pardon?"

47

"I've found I take on the qualities of dragons from myths and legends," he replied stiffly. "We like to hoard things. *I* like to hoard things."

An odd, tight feeling settled in Arabella's chest, a feeling she was unfamiliar with. It was an odd combination of fear and intrigue. No, not fear, she decided. She was fairly certain if Xavier had any intention of harming her, he would have done so already. Nervousness, perhaps and a little excitement. No one had ever wanted her before in the way she suspected he meant. She felt herself blush and hoped he didn't notice. Had she really been hurt when he'd grabbed her with his tail? "Am I a thing?" she asked.

He gave her a look that clearly questioned her intelligence. "Of course not. You know that. I'm merely explaining to you why your presence here has made me so discombobulated. I haven't spoken with humans about my condition before, let alone before I had to start shifting. Before I turned into what I am." He turned away and headed up the stairs.

Arabella was close at his heels. "You said you came here on an expedition."

"I did."

A scrap of a memory materialized in her mind, a bit of conversation she'd filed away before she left the Santiago airfield. "You were part of that lost expedition," she said, remembering the comptroller's warnings. "With those researchers."

He looked over his shoulder at her, brows raised, and Arabella knew she'd guessed correctly.

"What happened to the rest of the expedition?"

He shrugged. "I imagine they went back to England after a spell."

"And they just… left you here?"

"I'm sure it wasn't a difficult decision to make," he

48

replied. He'd reached the top of the stairs and held out a hand for her to help her up the steepest part.

She hesitated for half a second, remembering how his tail wrapped around her moments ago. *I didn't hate that.* She accepted it, noting how warm he was. A shiver rippled through her.

"Cold?" he asked.

"A little." It was technically part of the truth. She wasn't about to admit to him that his touch had any kind of effect on her.

He let her go, and she immediately missed it.

"We'll take a look at your dirigible tomorrow," he said abruptly. "See if we can't get you back in the clouds sooner rather than later. I don't want to leave it damaged in the open longer than necessary."

As much as Arabella missed the comfort of her dirigible, she thought she might miss Xavier's mountain, or at least the opportunity it presented. She wished he'd opened up to her more about his life. About his aborted Antarctic mission. "What kind of researcher were you?"

"Paleontology. I imagine some major discoveries have been made since I was last in England." A wistful expression crossed his face, and she thought he must miss his colleagues or laboratory, wherever a paleontologist conducted his work. It disappeared just as quickly. "I'll bid you goodnight now, Arabella."

So, he wanted to return to a semblance of their previous formality. She couldn't help but feel a stab of disappointment at that. Why, she couldn't say.

"Good night," she said, and returned to her room.

CHAPTER 7

*A*rabella's sleep was troubled. Images of the encounter with Xavier ran over and over on a loop in her mind like a zoetrope.

She descended the rough stairs to his lair. Took in the glittering walls, crusted with diamonds no one else in the world knew about. Saw him in his dragon form, gigantic and glorious, his scales glowing in the torchlight. Including the tail that wrapped itself around her in an act of possession that should have bothered her but didn't.

That was the part she kept coming back to, over and over.

In one version of the dream, he was in his human form, dressed in his threadbare clothes, his arms around her instead of his tail. His face leaned closer to hers. Arabella felt hers grow hot and her eyes closed in anticipation...

Only for her to wake up.

Her face was still warm and her body tingled with awareness. She didn't know if she would be able to look

Xavier in the eye for a while yet. He was the only person she had in her life at the moment, and he was determined to see her back to England as soon as possible. Or at least away from Antarctica, as long as she was far away from him. She hated that he wanted her away from him. She knew she had that effect on people but it still hurt. Arabella freshened up as best she could before making her way to what she was thinking of as the cave's foyer. The fire still blazed, giving off comfortable heat. "Xavier?" she called.

Silence greeted her.

She stuck her head in his room and noted it was empty. When she looked in the doorway to his lair, she saw it was dark, too. The cave felt empty, somehow, like she'd known subconsciously that he wasn't there. Disappointment thrummed in her. She missed him because of her dream, she reasoned. She'd had other dreams of the sort, usually much more explicit, about other men she'd met during her travels. That same wistfulness threaded through her when she woke up and remembered they weren't real.

There was something so much more disconcerting about this feeling and Xavier that she wasn't ready to address yet.

She helped herself to some dried penguin meat and, wrapped in a skin she sat in front of the fire to wait. Arabella refused to make herself look like any more of a fool than she already had or put both of them in danger again. She guessed half an hour had passed before Xavier stepped into the cave, triumph on his face. At the sight of his grin, Arabella couldn't keep one from forming on her face.

"I believe I've fixed your dirigible," he announced by way of greeting.

Time seemed to suspend itself for a moment. She felt

frozen in place in a way that had nothing to do with the cold. She felt her smile slowly fade away. "You did?"

"I still had parts from another one," he said. His expression faltered, and she wondered how he acquired them. "They were a match with your damaged components. The balloon has been re-inflated and I've moved it underneath a ledge to protect it from the elements. The storm has let up for a little while, but I'm sure it'll start up again soon. The weather is as good as it will get to take off."

It took a few seconds for the weight of Xavier's words to make their impact. "You mean I have to leave today?"

He nodded. "I checked your fuel reserves and you don't have quite enough to get you to Santiago on that power. You'll have to coast by with the balloon for at least two thousand miles, and you have to do that with clear weather. I don't have any excess fuel here and I don't know when you'll have another chance at leaving."

He held out his hand to her, and she accepted it. He hauled her to her feet. "I was going to coast anyway," she said. Doing so would take longer, but as Xavier pointed out, wind power saved fuel.

"If your dirigible is damaged again, I may not be able to repair it. You would be trapped here."

A strange, unfamiliar sense of loss twisted around her heart, as illogical as it was. Arabella didn't know why she felt this way. Xavier had made it abundantly clear since she crashed into his mountain that he didn't want her with him. Except for that bizarre possessive streak he'd shown a couple of times that sent an odd thrill through her whenever she thought about it. She knew the last thing Xavier truly wanted was for her to continue invading his space and reminded herself that his possession was the result of his dragon half, not his human side. Arabella had to listen to what the human and rational side of him wanted; she didn't belong here, in this frozen desert. She'd made it here, all the same. She realized for the first time that she had actually managed to visit all seven continents. It was a major milestone, and had done it by the time she was twenty-six, four years earlier than she originally intended.

All of this was still something she could be proud of.

It was time for her to leave, to return to England and figure out what to do next. "I understand," she said, finally answering Xavier. "Let me get my things and I'll be ready to leave."

She was true to her word, and in a few moments, followed Xavier out of the cave, into the blistering cold. The storm had died down through the night, leaving an endless white landscape before them. She stayed close to Xavier, knowing that if she dawdled or wandered away, she would never be able to find her way back to the cave or her dirigible.

As he promised, the dirigible was stowed under what looked to be a rock shelf jutting from the mountain, covered with snow. Its balloon was inflated and upright, the vessel's body sporting new patched in a few places. "How did you do this?" Arabella asked in wonder.

"I told you I had the components." His voice was raised so she could hear him better over the ever-present wind, and she detected pride in it. "It wasn't that difficult once I moved your dirigible from the crash site. It was a straightforward repair once I got it out of the snow. You haven't had any fuel line breaks or other fatal damage."

"How the hell did you haul..." She realized how. "You did it in your dragon form."

"I did."

They walked under the ledge to the dirigible's lower exterior door, still locked. Arabella didn't have the keys, nor did she have a platform that would take her to the deck area and allow her to enter it that way. "Damn," she muttered. She wondered if Xavier would shift and let her ride on his back to the deck.

He picked up on her quandary right away. "This is a puzzle lock."

She nodded. "In case I wasn't in possession of my keys." She felt herself flush with embarrassment. "I—I have never forgotten my keys, and I can't remember the puzzle offhand. My father set it." It was yet one more stupid thing she had overlooked during this whole ordeal.

"No worries about that." Xavier pressed his ear against the door and twirled the lock's levers, rearranged its pieces, his eyes closed in concentration. After a few minutes of trying different solutions, his face relaxed and he unlocked the door. He held it open, as gallant a gesture as a man leading her to a dance floor.

Not that Arabella was the sort to be invited to those kinds of soirees. She wondered if Xavier was in his old life. Once inside the dirigible's belly, she set about switching on the flameless torches installed along the walls. She was relieved to see they operated none the worse for wear after the crash. In the dim lighting, she could see that the place was in disarray, but nothing seemed to be severely damaged. She would have more than enough time once she hit the wind to clean up. She unhooked one of the torches and made her way to the flight deck, Xavier closely behind her. The light picked up just how much of a mess she had on her hands, and she sighed. She hated housework. To her surprise, the deck was clear of snow and ice. She turned to Xavier. "How did you get the snow swept away so quickly?"

Color touched his cheeks. "I melted it off."

Arabella couldn't tell if it was the dim light afforded to them or if she was projecting her own exhaustion, but he looked more tired than she'd ever seen him. Dark shadows pooled under his eyes, and she realized he had to have been working since she went to sleep. All night, into the day. Whatever time it happened to be. She'd lost track of it.

"You breathed fire on my wooden deck to melt the snow," she said.

"I didn't burn anything."

"I'm sure you knew exactly what you were doing." She appreciated his careful efforts, but hurt inexplicably pricked at her. He wanted her gone.

Xavier nodded. "I'll help you take off."

Arabella looked pointedly at the steering yoke. "There's only enough room for one captain."

"No, I'll pull your dirigible out from underneath the ledge," he explained. "You'll need help with takeoff." He looked around the flight box. "A little privacy, please?"

Not for the first time, she felt like an idiot. Of course, he would do that in his dragon form. She nodded and motioned to turn around. There was one more thing she wanted to do before he changed into his dragon form and she never saw him again. She threw her arms around him in a fierce hug, noting he smelled faintly of smoke. She liked it. "Thank you for everything you've done for me." He stiffened for a few seconds before he returned the gesture, strong arms circling her in a way that reminded him of his dragon tail. Her face heated.

"Thank you for providing some company," he replied.

"I made things worse for you."

He shrugged. "It was nice to find out that I haven't entirely lost my manners after all these years, and you

55

brought tea. I'll think of you every time I boil water for a cup."

She smiled and willed back tears that had unexpectedly formed. When he pulled away and regarded her in silence for a moment, she hoped he didn't notice them. If he did, he didn't let on. His eyes never leaving her face, he tucked an errant strand of her hair that escaped from her braid behind her ear. A thrill coursed through her at the small contact and with it, sadness that it wouldn't happen again. Arabella's gaze met his and held it. Why, she wasn't sure.

Xavier squeezed her hand through her glove in a gesture she guessed was supposed to be affectionate. "I'll shift now and then we'll get you airborne."

THE UNEXPECTED SADNESS that clung to Xavier like a second skin was shed as he changed into his dragon form. It was replaced by determination, a need to show Arabella that he could force her dirigible into the air. A need to see her off as safely as he could. It took some maneuvering to haul the dirigible out from underneath the rock shelf with his teeth and claws. It was certainly more difficult than moving it there in the first place but it slid out along the snow. He was relieved to see the repaired balloon was still intact and inflated after scraping the rock.

Arabella activated the dirigible's engine, then activated the helium chamber. The vessel struggled, shaking from disuse and the cold. Xavier held his breath expectantly, grateful that her dirigible's balloon was helium-powered instead of hydrogen. That particular gas wasn't one that a fire-breathing dragon wanted to be near.

Especially when someone like Arabella was involved.

There's that sadness again. He damned himself for it.

56

Arabella Greaves was an intrusion. If she stayed here much longer, someone would come looking for her and might well find him. It was best for everyone that she leave. He had been alone for years before she crashed into his mountain. He would survive after she left.

Then why was there a dull ache in his chest when he thought about her sailing away?

He ignored it and focused on the dirigible. It raised itself a few yards in the air, just enough for Xavier to nudge his head underneath it and lift it higher. The vessel raised again, and Xavier crawled beneath it, bolstering it into the air as best as he could. He struggled a little to free his wings enough to take flight, but managed after a moment. He hoped he hadn't frightened Arabella too badly.

Hell, she had flown all the way to Antarctica on her own. He doubted a little rocking from a dragon beneath her dirigible would faze her.

Still, he wished he could apologize for the discomfort. Speaking of discomfort... His body screamed in protest as he realized the weight of the vessel above him. Even though the snow had stopped falling, the wind was still fierce and he had to rapidly blink to clear his eyes of tears.

I've ever experienced that before. I didn't know my eyes could water in my dragon form!

If he still kept a diary, he would have noted that. The dirigible heaved upward, finally taking flight, and sailed with the wind. Xavier's heart leapt, proud of Arabella for the successful launch. It was for the best that she was leaving. He reminded himself if she stayed, someone would come looking for her. It wouldn't be untoward to fly alongside her for a little while, just until she got used to the freezing skies again. He moved out from under the dirigible and stretched his aching wings before taking full flight. Keeping pace with the dirigible's deck, he spotted

Arabella at the steering yoke in the flight box, her expression serious, focused on the journey ahead.

Her gaze met his and a smile bloomed across her face.

Xavier would miss that. His mind flashed back to the night before, when his tail snaked out and... Shame welled in him at the memory. The compulsive need to plunder and hoard meant he couldn't rejoin polite society. What he had done to Arabella marked the first and only time that had happened, and he didn't dare risk a repeat. He soared upward to match the dirigible's trajectory. Mild alarm threaded through him when he saw the speed Arabella had picked up so quickly, but he didn't interfere. He just sailed alongside her, content to have something in common with her before she left Antarctica forever.

A quick glance at the flight box showed her face to be in deep concentration, but she didn't look nervous. Xavier decided he wouldn't be, either.

A gust of wind nearly halted him in his path. The dirigible's balloon tilted to starboard, but Arabella immediately righted the vessel. Buoyed by helium and wind power, the dirigible picked up speed at a near-frightening rate, and Xavier found himself struggling to keep up. He looked down at the ground and flinched. He couldn't remember when he last flew at this height. For the first time since he discovered he was a dragon, he felt nauseous looking at the frozen landscape.

How quickly can her dirigible get this high?

For the first time, he was flummoxed at how technology had advanced in just five short years. The dirigible that brought him here... A wave of nausea roiled over him in a way that had nothing to do with nervousness around heights. He didn't want to think about that journey. Not now, not ever. He still forged on, determined to see Arabella off as long as he could hold out. As he sailed alongside her, he began to fully appreciate her skill as a pilot.

She had chalked up her crash as a fluke caused by the weather.

Seeing how she navigated through powerful gusts of wind and the snow that had started to fall again, he finally believed her. She would have been an absolute force to be reckoned with in any location outside of Antarctica. Wind heaved at him and the dirigible, harder than any gust he'd ever felt before. His body sailed upward against its will and he struggled in vain to right himself. He lurched left, striking the side of the dirigible, before being launched upward again into what looked like a vortex of swirling snow. The wind knocked the air from him. He couldn't see the ground. When he looked to his side, he realized he couldn't see the dirigible, either, even though he could hear its engine faintly over the roaring wind in his ears. The wind slammed him headfirst into something hard and immobile. He couldn't see what it was, and as he lost consciousness, he found he didn't care.

His last thought before slipping into oblivion was hope that Arabella would make it to Santiago in one piece.

ARABELLA'S CONCENTRATION was broken by the gigantic, scaled body of a dragon slamming into her dirigible's flight box and then to the exposed deck. She screamed, the sound bouncing off its glass walls. "Xavier!" she yelped.

He wasn't moving, nor had he shifted back into his human form. Terror and indecision clawed at her as she mulled over her options to save him.

She couldn't go back to ground. According to her instruments, she was over ten thousand feet in the air. She didn't know where she could safely land and if she did, she was unsure if she could get her dirigible airborne again. She had nearly reached the perfect altitude to take her away from this frozen hellscape back to civilization. It still wasn't safe to drag Xavier into the relative warmth of the lower deck, and she wasn't strong enough to do so, besides. She would have to wait until he shifted.

If he shifted.

Tears of frustration clouded her vision. She impatiently brushed them away with a gloved hand.

What if he had died?

Why the hell had he collapsed in the first place?

The dirigible arced upward. Xavier remained pinned to the deck, his body against the glass as it surged. According to her flight instruments, she was nearly at cruising altitude. Once she was finally among the clouds, she would shut off power to the engine. The helium and balloon would take over, guided by the wind to take her to Santiago and from there, back to England. That added another quandary to her situation. To Xavier's situation.

Like it or not, he was coming with her.

As soon as the dirigible reached the clouds and settled into its new course, she was ready to save him as best she could. Arabella tied a rescue rope around her waist, a safety feature she had never had to use before. No one had ever had to conduct exterior repairs while in the air, or been in danger of being blown overboard. She was pleasantly surprised when she cautiously opened the flight box's door to the deck. The wind was far less ferocious at these heights, although the cold still reached her bones. She was grateful for the rope as she shook Xavier where she guessed his shoulder would be. "Wake up!" she shouted into one scaled ear.

He snorted a little. Relief flowed through her at the

sign of life. Relief and concern. He was capable of breathing fire, after all.

"Xavier!" She shook him again. "If you cough and set fire to my dirigible, I'm going to be very cross with you!"

He grunted again.

"Wake up!" She nudged him with a booted toe. "Or at least shift so I can drag you below decks!"

His eyes opened, but the pupils were glassy, unfocused. Arabella knew little of medicine, let alone medicine for dragons, but she could tell that was a bad sign. Had he hit his head when he collapsed?

He opened them wider, as if finally in recognition. He opened his mouth, revealing rows of sharp fangs, before his eyes rolled back in his head. He began to shake and his scales started to melt away. His body rearranged itself, naked skin and limbs appearing.

Arabella could have wept at the sight. As it was, she didn't want her eyes to freeze shut, so she willed the tears away. As soon as he was back in his human form, laying on his back, she grabbed his hands and dragged him into the flight box. From there, she summoned all her strength and as carefully as she could, hauled him into her cozy cabin belowdecks.

HE WAS WARM.

Xavier stretched and snuggled a little deeper beneath the blanket. He couldn't remember the last time he felt this warm. It was pleasant. He missed it. He was warm and he could smell a familiar, sugary odor that he couldn't immediately place. It wasn't biscuits just out of the oven, but a little more clinical. Almost medicinal.

Dr. Thaddeus's Miracle Elixir.

The thought of the stupid sugar water placebo Arabella favored had him fully awake, and he took in his surroundings with horror. He laid in an unfamiliar bed. It was a small one, pushed against the wall, but a bed nonetheless. He had blankets heaped over him that bore a distinctive trace of Arabella Greaves's scent, without a penguin skin to be seen. Arabella herself stood next to the bed, an unstopped bottle of the alleged miracle elixir in one hand and a spoon in the other. It looked to be silver. Xavier's dragon side itched to snatch it from her. They stared at each other for a few seconds.

Arabella's expression was unreadable.

Xavier tried to make his the same. Inside, he felt an odd mixture of relief and fury. She was safe. She'd made it away from Antarctica in one piece. She'd brought him with her. "What the everloving hell is this?" he bit out at last.

She flushed in the light offered by the flameless torch on the wall. "I'm sure you have many questions." She looked at the bottle in her hand. "You left this bottle behind when you ransacked my cupboards."

"Arabella, what is this?"

"I found half a tin of tea you left, too. We'll have to ration it. It's all we have until we get to Santiago." She poured a small measure of elixir into the spoon. "I'm sure you have a headache. This will help."

"Arabella!" He didn't intend to shout. He immediately regretted it when he saw her flinch. She took advantage of the opportunity to shove the spoon into his mouth. He swallowed it—ugh, too sweet—and waited for her explanation.

She yelled right back at him. "You collapsed on my fucking deck! You fell out of the sky! What was I supposed to do, shove you off? I saved your life!" She stoppered the

62

bottle and slammed it on a shelf fastened to the wall. "I suppose we're now even."

"How the hell are we even?" He threw back the blankets. Arabella looked scandalized at the sight and he remembered he was naked. He quickly rearranged them back over his body.

It was nice to be lying in a proper bed. Even nicer that it smelled like Arabella. Not that he would ever admit that to her.

"You saved my life when I fell out of the sky," she reminded him.

He immediately felt like an idiot. She was right, damn it.

"How did you manage that?" she demanded.

"You were there when I rescued you."

She gave him a withering look. "I mean, how did you manage to fall out of the sky?"

"I don't know, and I don't want to think about that now." He changed the subject. "You can't really mean to take me to Santiago."

"I can and I do. I'm not going back to Antarctica. If you want to go back to Mount Xavier, you'll have to find someone in Santiago to take you." She crossed her arms over her chest in defiance. "I'm not going back there. You're welcome to stay with me, but I fully intend on returning to England."

Dread sawed at him. He knew there was no practical way he could return to Antarctica short of sneaking his way on to an expedition. He wouldn't be able to fly that far on his own power, nor did he have the means to purchase a ticket aboard a ship or dirigible. He thought about his lair, so carefully carved into his mountain, his hoard of diamonds glittering in his cavern, and of the tea he'd saved from Arabella's dirigible. He would never be able to return to his treasures. He eyed the spoon still in Arabella's hand. He snatched it and stuck it under the blanket. "I'm keeping this."

"Of course, you are," she snapped. "If you decide you want to discuss this rationally, come and speak to me. I won't be far." She stomped out of the room, slamming the door behind her.

CHAPTER 8

*A*rabella adjusted the fur blanket around herself and gritted her teeth. She took a sip from her tea and silently cursed the idiot dragon holed up in her cabin. He would certainly be warmer than she was right now, huddled in her bed under a mountain of covers while she was in the flight box. Ordinarily, she would be content to let the dirigible follow its course, letting the wind and helium balloon work together to propel it. She'd lost some faith in her navigation abilities since she crashed.

Every comptroller she had ever spoken to along her trek to Antarctica had been correct about the foolishness of her endeavor.

Xavier was, too.

She was supremely lucky to be alive, and refused to take any more chances with her safety until they landed in Santiago, which meant she hadn't slept despite the late hour. *Their* safety, she reminded herself. Xavier was her responsibility for as long as he remained on her dirigible. They hadn't spoken since he took possession of the spoon and he hadn't left her room, let alone the cabin. At least

65

needing to keep an eye on the skies meant she had an excuse not to go belowdecks, as chilled as she was. There was a peacefulness to be found behind the steering yoke, a return to her ordinary life that was a relief. Her thoughts were interrupted by the sound of feet climbing the stairs to the flight box. She closed her eyes and uttered a silent prayer to the powers above that Xavier wasn't going to try to make off with her fur blanket.

His throat cleared behind her. "Arabella."

She sighed and kept her gaze on the deck. "The only options I had were taking you with me or pushing you off the dirigible."

"I know." She heard him shuffling behind her. "It's past midnight."

A clock was affixed to the steering yoke. Arabella knew full well the time. "I'd prefer to stay here until we've reached less windy skies. I'm still nervous about this part of the flight over the Antarctic Ocean." She looked over her shoulder at him, wrapped head to toe in the blankets from her bed. His hair was mussed from sleep. "You should go back to bed. You had a hell of a fall."

"Arabella…"

"I don't have the energy to get yelled at for saving you."

"I've had some time to think about it. I'm not angry. You did what any reasonable and kind person would do for someone who flew too high and lost consciousness."

"Is that what happened?"

He nodded. "I think so. I've never reached those heights in my dragon form. I don't know why it happened."

"All right. Well, you're welcome to return to Antarctica when we've reached Santiago. I can give you the money for a ticket," she said.

"No, thank you."

"You don't mean to fly back there yourself? It isn't possible."

"No, I wouldn't be able to board another dirigible legally. I don't have a passport anymore, and no means of procuring a new one. Which reminds me: when we arrive in Santiago, I can't leave your dirigible." He leaned against the glass wall, his expression dejected. "I have to return to England. It's the least worst option for me right now."

"Where will you go?"

He shrugged and pulled the blankets tighter around himself. "I'm sure I'll be able to secure another position with a university or in a lab. I'll sort it out later."

His words were a surprise to Arabella. "What about your dragon?"

"What about it?" he countered. "I'm in an untenable position at the moment. I'll need funds to start my life over in another remote place. Working in academia is all I know what to do. I can save for a while for passage somewhere, or join an expedition and get lost."

"The same way you did when you arrived in Antarctica?"

His expression shuttered.

It was as if Arabella had watched a factory shut down for the night: the lights turned down, doors slammed and locked shut. Her heart thudded in her ears and she wondered if she had gone too far.

A muscle in his jaw ticked. "Yes," he said shortly. His voice was calm, but there were undercurrents of anger and shame in that single word.

"Couldn't you stay somewhere remote in Britain? Surely, there's a moor or hill that would suit your purposes."

"I appreciate your suggestions." He stared straight

ahead as the snowflakes whipped against the flight box walls. "But have you considered that I've thought about all my options, long before you knew dragons existed?"

She hadn't. "I suppose not. I'll shut up now."

He sighed. "Damn it, Arabella." He looked like he wanted to say something else but his lips thinned. He shook his head.

She changed the subject. "How are you feeling? Besides being angry and anxious, I mean. How's your head?"

"I have some bruises, but they'll heal quickly. I don't have any head injuries as far as I can tell."

"Well, you have that spoon I left the bottle of Dr. Thaddeus in the cabin. Help yourself," she said.

Once again, he looked like he wanted to say something but talked himself out of it. When he spoke, his voice was quiet, almost placated. "Thank you."

"We should be clear of this weather within the next twelve hours. I expect we'll land in Santiago in two days, if not sooner. Once we're out of this wind and snow, I'll let the wind take over and I can take a nap."

"I can pilot," he offered.

"No, you can't." It was at the tip of her tongue to remind him that the last time he was aboard a dirigible, it crashed. She didn't know the details other than that, and didn't want to alienate him further. "It's been a while for you," she amended. "I wouldn't feel comfortable leaving the yoke in someone else's hands right now. Perhaps when we leave Santiago and we're in friendlier skies, I can show you a few things."

His teeth chattered in response. "All right."

"For God's sake, go back downstairs. You'll catch your death out here."

"No, I won't. I'm better suited to the cold than humans are."

"And yet here you stand before me, shivering. You're not totally impervious to it, and you're injured, besides. Go back to sleep. I'm the captain of this vessel. That's an order."

His nostrils flared, and she remembered again what a powerful creature he was but he didn't argue. "I'll have some of your medicine, if it'll make you feel better."

"You're the one who's hurt."

"But the medicine's important to you."

Irritation welled in her, and she no longer had the patience to try to talk some sense into him. "Xavier, just go back to bed," she snapped. "We'll discuss all of this when we're both better rested."

He sighed again, but didn't offer a retort. He turned around and descended the stairs, leaving her alone in the flight box with her thoughts.

THE NEXT FOUR days were spent with Xavier and Arabella keeping their interactions to a minimum. Xavier offered to return her bedroom to her but she demurred, insisting he needed it more. She took a couple of naps during the daytime after their first night of travel, fitfully sleeping on the lounge's sofa. When Xavier dared to venture to the galley during those times, he could tell she wasn't truly sleeping. She looked so uncomfortable, with her long legs scrunched up on the sofa, hands tucked beneath the thin decorative pillow under her head.

Guilt chewed at him. Guilt, shame, anger, and fear of the unknown ahead. His blustering about academic positions aside, he was truly at a loss for how he was going to continue living once they reached England.

You forgot to add 'lust' to that list.

The reminder popped into his head as he crept past a sleeping Arabella to the dirigible's galley. He didn't touch the scant tea leaves in their tin and instead used the sink's pump to pour some water in a cup. Lust. There was that, too. His physical attraction to her was frustrating and unwanted. It was yet another reason he avoided her as best he could, for fear he would make an idiot out of himself. It was so difficult to be dignified and put together when one didn't have any clothes and had to stay covered up in a sheet or blanket. He'd even checked Arabella's closet out of desperation and found she had nothing that would fit him.

She was nearly as tall as he was, and slender. Her flight clothes were tailored for her, with hardly an inch of fabric to spare. She didn't have so much as an oversized shirt he could borrow, not even a nightgown.

That was curious, but he preferred not to dwell on why she might not own one.

In bare feet, he shuffled back to the bedroom, cup and a fork in hand. He told himself he would return the fork as soon as he got bored with it. It had been sitting in the tiny sink, left over from when he and Arabella had shared a couple of her hardtack biscuits for their evening meal the night before. She had used utensils to carve off crumbly bits and delicately eaten them.

Neither of them had spoken much. The silence, save for the hum of the dirigible's helium engine, had been nearly deafening. Xavier hadn't known he could be unnerved by it after being the only human in Antarctica for so long.

Arabella shifted on the sofa. "Xavier."

He paused, bedsheet wrapped around his waist. "Yes?"

"Do I want to ask why you have a fork?"

He looked down at it, the possessiveness over it, the need to hide it under the mattress with the spoon more powerful than his embarrassment. "Why do you think I have it?"

She sighed and stood up, still wearing her flight trousers and jacket. She tucked locks of red hair that escaped their braid behind her ears. She looked exhausted. "I have some jewelry aboard that belonged to my mother. Perhaps you can make a game of it and find it. It's hidden."

"Why would it have to be hidden?" Xavier ignored his piqued interest in hunting for the jewelry.

"So my father's wife doesn't find it and keep it for herself. She doesn't have the excuse of being a dragon for her actions." She tugged at the end of her red braid, messy from sleep. She sighed again, unfastened it, and worked her fingers through her hair. She began to braid it again. "I will require the jewelry to be returned to me at some point, but if it will keep you from total boredom, search the cabin for it." She slipped a watch from her trouser pocket and glanced at its face. "I'm returning to the deck. We'll be in Santiago in less than twelve hours. I only want to stay there long enough to replenish the fuel and pick up some supplies." She gave a pointed look at his bedsheet toga. "You need clothing."

He tried not to let her loose hair distract him, but it was difficult. "I suppose you want your bed back, too."

"You've been injured. I'll be fine sleeping on the sofa until we get back to England. It's only for another few days. We just have to get to Santiago and I can get some proper sleep." She tied off the end of her braid with a ribbon. "You'd best start looking for that jewelry if you want to keep yourself from going mad with boredom."

"What kind of jewelry is it?"

She gave him a look that clearly questioned his intelligence. "I don't have any of it on my person or in a box in my bedroom. You'll know it when you see it." She sighed. "There's a necklace with a ruby pendant and a matching pair of earbobs. They're genuine and were handed down from my great-grandmother. There's also a small assortment of paste jewelry that my mother was very fond of and wore every day."

"What do I get if I can't keep the jewelry?" Xavier asked. "I know you won't want me to keep it."

"What do you want?"

Xavier's mouth unexpectedly went dry at the question. He knew she probably wouldn't appreciate the answer.

Her. I want her.

"Uh," he said, his mind working frantically. "I suppose I get to indulge my dragon's needs to plunder." Perhaps she would let him hang on to a paste-filled bracelet. Even if she didn't, Xavier was still amenable to a treasure hunt for the sake of it.

"Don't plunder my walls, floorboards, or pipes," Arabella said. "Don't tear into or break anything."

"I won't, and I'll find them by the end of the day," he promised.

"They're not in my mattress, either."

The mention of her mattress brought other images to mind that she likely wouldn't appreciate. "I assumed the mattress would fall under things not to tear into."

"I wasn't sure if dragons would be compelled to do such things," she said.

He shrugged. "It's not the same as hoarding anything shiny and sparkling." Already, he missed his diamond-filled underground lair in Antarctica. He tried not to think about how he would likely not be able to return. If he fell out of a South Pole-bound dirigible again, it would set off even more suspicions than the ones he would be raising when he returned to London. He forced himself to focus on the challenge ahead of him. It wouldn't provide the same thrill as carving out a space for himself in a mountain, but it would have to do. He tried not to think about how he would cope with his dragon's need to plunder and hoard when he returned to England.

The South Kensington Museum is full of jewels.

He deliberately hadn't set foot in that museum since he learned he was a dragon shifter. The thought of all the gold and sapphires on display made his teeth and gums itch.

"Xavier?" Arabella's voice was curious. "You look a little feral. And it isn't just the hair."

He blinked, trying to force his mind back to the task at hand. *Arabella's mother's jewelry. Hidden somewhere on the dirigible. Find it. Perhaps she'll let you keep a piece as a token of her appreciation.* His gaze met hers. "Feral?" He touched his hair. It was longer than was considered fashionable, but he kept it as tidy as he could. Albeit he cut it with a pocketknife he'd had on himself when he first arrived in Antarctica. Of course, that pocketknife was now lost forever.

"You're missing your spectacles, too."

Irritation rankled him. "I'll get another set when we return to England and I'm wearing your bedsheet, too. Is there anything else you wish to criticize about my appearance?"

Her face crumpled for a second, and he thought she was about to cry. Just as quickly, she smoothed her expression. "No, and I apologize. I'm feeling out of sorts."

73

"I'm familiar with that," he replied dryly.

"It's nothing personal. Please, look for the jewelry if it will give you something to do. Help yourself to Dr. Thaddeus's Miracle Elixir. I can tell it's working. You're up and about and grumpy as usual."

He wasn't going to argue over the lack of efficacy of the elixir she loved so much. It was time that had healed him. Time and his dragon physiology. "You should help yourself to a cup of tea," he urged her. "Before you go back to the deck."

She nodded. "That sounds ideal."

He waited until she had prepared her tea, then watched as she climbed the narrow stairs to the deck. He looked around the small living space, anticipation running hotly through his veins.

There was jewelry to be found here, somewhere.

CHAPTER 9

The Santiago comptroller on duty was the same man Arabella spoke to before taking her final leg of her Antarctic journey. Like the comptroller in New York, he had tried to talk her out of it. It took a few seconds for him to recognize her, his eyebrows raised. He was clearly surprised to see her alive. He'd been the nicest comptroller she'd fought with during this trip, she recalled. He'd said goodbye to her with an obvious trace of sadness on his face. Undoubtedly, he was sure that the next time he heard of her, it would be on a missing persons telegram or poster stuck to the Santiago airfield office's walls.

"Look who's back!" the comptroller exclaimed in Spanish.

Arabella replied in kind. "It wasn't easy."

"You made it there?" he asked incredulously.

She nodded. "Just barely. I didn't stay too long."

The comptroller leaned back in his chair and tented his fingers. His left eye was clockwork-powered and a tiny gear on it whirred as he regarded Arabella with respect. "And your dirigible is in one piece?"

She nodded.

"God protects saints and fools."

"I'm sure I fall into the 'fool' category."

That earned a laugh from him. "Would you be offended if I agreed with you?"

"Not at all. No one should try what I did. It's sheer dumb luck that I'm still alive."

"Perhaps you'll join a guided expedition group next time," he suggested. He riffled through some papers on the desk before him. "I'm certain I have a handbill or two around here."

She shook her head. "No, thank you. I won't be returning to Antarctica again." The thought of ever traversing that stormy weather again brought more chills to her than the Antarctic winds ever did. It also tore out a small piece of her heart to imagine Xavier returning to that place, alone again for God knew how many years. He'd been lonely in his self-imposed exile. If he couldn't be with other dragons, perhaps he would be satisfied with understanding humans, at least for a spell.

The comptroller changed the subject back to her return journey. "Will you be going back to England the same way you arrived?"

She nodded. "Yes, I'll be flying to Havana next. I'd like to leave tomorrow morning." It was only half-past nine in the evening, but she was already looking forward to that night's sleep.

He nodded and set about plugging in her details to the telegraph machine in front of him. "I'll notify the Havana flight office immediately. When do you expect you'll be there?"

"Tomorrow afternoon. It won't be a long stay, just enough to check my equipment when we've reached the northern hemisphere."

"Your balloon doesn't like the changes in temperature so quickly?"

"No. I want to make sure it won't give me any difficulty when I cross the Atlantic."

"Good plan." The comptroller kept his natural and clockwork eyes on the telegraph machine. "All right, Miss Greaves. The Havana flight office has been notified of your arrival. If there are any changes made to your itinerary before you sail tomorrow, a messenger will be sent to your dock. Is there anything else I can help you with?"

"Yes. I'm in need of some dry goods. Where's the best place to buy some ready-made clothes and housewares?"

"We have a mercantile on site," the comptroller replied. "It's at the airfield entrance, inside the gate. It's about a ten-minute walk from here. Do you have any hard currency on you?"

"American dollars and pounds sterling."

"Neither will be good there. I can exchange some dollars to pesos for you now."

Once again, Arabella realized she'd been caught short and rescued by someone with more foresight than she had. "Thank you."

He made the transaction, and Arabella thanked him before leaving the office.

She found the mercantile without any difficulty. There was little to be found in terms of fashionable men's clothing, but she doubted Xavier cared too much about fashion at this point. She picked out some practical men's clothing, sturdy boots, tins of tea and packages of chocolate. She spied piles of used books in various languages in a large wooden bin and impulsively picked through it. He needed something to entertain himself once he sniffed out her mother's jewelry stashed in a cloth bag in the sofa's supports.

One cover caught her eye: *Beneath the Dark Waves.* It wasn't just the title that snared her attention, it was the author's name. Lucien Quinn. The man who rented her family's ancestral estate in Gull's End and nearly destroyed it, all while living in sin with a mysterious woman who claimed to be his cousin. A woman the mad people of Gull's End claimed was a mermaid.

She turned the book over in her hands. She'd once promised Lucien in a letter that she would read one of his novels. She hadn't done so yet; finding the novel so far away from England might well be a sign. She added it to her pile of things. Her arms were full when she left the mercantile. Xavier looked at her with curiosity when she returned to the dirigible.

"What's all that?"

She opened the giant package and unpacked everything. "The clothes will keep you decent until we get to England. Were you one for fashion when you were last there?"

He shrugged. "If it wasn't part of my academic interests, I didn't pay much attention to it, fashion included."

"I didn't have any academic interests before I was expelled from finishing school and I still don't care about fashion." She was fifteen was she was deemed to be impossible to mold into a lady.

He picked up the novel. "What's this?"

"That was written by the man who rented my family's estate. The one who may have married the mermaid."

"You didn't tell me it was Lucien Quinn." He opened the book to the first page. "I'm surprised you found an English novel here."

"You've heard of him?" She was surprised.

"He isn't exactly an obscure novelist."

"There was a whole pile of used books for sale at the

airfield mercantile. In all languages. This is a popular flight port," she said.

"Have you read any of his books?"

"I'm not much of a reader." She shrugged.

He looked at her like she had two heads. "I see."

"Not everyone is cut out for a life in laboratories and academia," she reminded him. "However, in my last letter to Mr. Quinn after the house's ballroom was flooded, I promised to read one of his books someday. That one will suffice." She noticed that Xavier didn't let go of the novel. If anything, his grip increased on it. "Are you going to hide that under the mattress?" she asked.

He held it to his chest protectively. "No."

"Liar."

That earned a smile from him.

Arabella ignored the flip-flop in her heart at the sight. "Did you find my mother's jewelry?"

He picked up the black velvet bag she hadn't noticed sitting on the sofa. "Far too easily. There are better places to hide things aboard this vessel."

"My father's wife wouldn't stoop to looking under furniture. It might wrinkle her skirt."

He handed it to her. She opened it and looked at the pieces inside. She could tell from the hungry look on his face that he wanted something. She picked out a silver ring too large for her fingers, a blue paste gem in the center, and pressed it into his palm. "You can keep this."

He didn't take it right away. "Are you certain?"

"I know you wanted to keep something. Keep this safe. Does it count as treasure if it was given to you?"

His hand curled around the ring. "I think so."

"Well, now you have something to start your hoard over with."

He opened his hand, stared at the ring, then at her with

an intensity that made her shiver. "I will guard this with my life. Thank you."

"I'd still like to read that novel."

"Of course."

An awkward silence that Arabella couldn't explain descended over them. "I think I'll get some sleep."

He immediately took the hint. "Understood. It's been a long journey."

"I'll see you in the morning," she said.

He nodded. "Sleep well."

ARABELLA TOOK in a deep breath of humid air and surveyed the early Havana evening from her dirigible's deck. This was certainly the prettiest airfield she'd ever docked in. There were planters full of brightly colored flowers lined the stone walkways between docking platforms, interspersed with occasional ironwood trees. The airfield comptroller's office building was painted a cheerful green, with a barrel tile roof and more flowers in front. The sun was setting, bathing the landscape in shades of pink and orange. It was one of the most beautiful sights she'd ever seen.

It was early evening when her dirigible was secured in place and she checked in with the comptroller's office. Her growling stomach told her it was time for supper. She couldn't face another meal of hardtack biscuits scraped apart with a knife and fork. She had landed at one of her favorite airfields in the world, an airfield surrounded by restaurants that had far more than terrible old hardtack on their menus. She retreated into the dirigible's belly to find Xavier. "I'm buying us some real food," she announced.

"You bought some real food in Santiago shortly before we took off."

"We sucked that down in about a day and a half," she replied. It was the first proper meal Xavier had had in years following his diet of penguin meat. She hadn't admitted as much at the time, but it was heartening to see him tuck into pastel de Choclo and ajiaco with as much gusto as he had. She'd brought back what she thought was enough food for an army before they launched back into the sky, but she'd severely underestimated his appetite. "What kind of supper are you feeling tonight?"

"I've been eating penguins for the last five years," he said, echoing her earlier thoughts. "I'm not particular. I trust your judgement."

She left the airfield and turned into the first restaurant she saw that catered to aviators. Arabella returned to the dirigible bearing paper boxes full of ropa vieja, yuca con mojo, rice and beans, and churros. She left them in the flight box before heading belowdecks to find Xavier, who was reading the novel she'd found in Santiago. "Let's eat outside. It would be a shame if you missed this sunset." She collected plates and utensils from the galley cupboard.

He hesitated for a half a second before saying, "All right."

Arabella spread out mats on the wooden deck that she kept in the flight box for such a purpose, then arranged the boxes on them. Xavier was unfazed by the food, instead transfixed by the airfield below them and Havana just beyond. "Xavier?" she asked curiously.

"Don't mind me," he said without looking at her. He gripped the railing, as if he were afraid he might be thrown overboard.

She thought she could hear a lump in his throat. Her

heart leapt to hers. She hoped she hadn't made another misstep with him.

"This is the first time I've seen civilization up close in five years," he finally said.

Arabella wasn't sure how to answer that. "Have you been to Havana before?" Immediately, she felt like an idiot. He likely had, on his way to Antarctica.

He surprised her. "No. During my last time aboard a dirigible, we made a stop in Buenos Aires before Santiago."

She remained fixed to the deck, knees tucked under her, waiting for him to join her.

He did, after another few moments collecting himself. "What's for supper? It smells amazing."

She opened the boxes to show him, unable to hide a smile when she saw his expression. He seemed to remember where he was before he could start drooling. "Thank you."

They served themselves and ate in silence while questions bounced around Arabella's mind about her passenger. "How's the novel?"

He shrugged. "Lucien Quinn's a tad melodramatic, but he tells a good tale. One could almost believe that sea monsters are real."

"I told you that the entire village of Gull's End is convinced that he's married to a mermaid."

"Given my shifting and fire-breathing existence, I don't see how mermaids couldn't possibly exist."

He'd already said as much. Arabella tried another tack. "I wish you had a passport so you could leave the dirigible and explore the city with me."

He looked surprised to hear that confession, but didn't comment on it. "I thought you wanted to return to England as soon as possible."

"I don't but I have nowhere else to return to, and I have to inform my father that I survived Antarctica."

"Inform or gloat?"

She paused, a forkful of ropa vieja a couple of inches from her lips as she considered his question. "Both."

"How many people told you that such a journey was foolish?"

"Everyone did. Were you told as much before you set sail?"

"Of course not. I was with an expedition." Now it was his turn to hesitate, as if he wanted to tell her something important.

Arabella resisted the urge to lean forward in anticipation. Her heart thundered, certain he was about to tell her something important.

Her instincts proved right. "I couldn't stay in England when I realized what I am," he said. "It was getting more and more difficult hiding my shifting and the urge to take anything shiny or sparkling. I was worried I would break into a museum or aristocrat's home or hurt someone. I fit into society less and less, even for an academic."

"Why would an academic not fit in?"

"I'm not a charming academic. You may have noticed that. My social skills kept declining. I didn't see the point in living as a human anymore."

"But you are," she protested. "You're still very much human. You would have killed me when I crashed into your mountain otherwise."

"I considered it," he confessed. His voice dropped to a whisper, tinged with shame.

Arabella wasn't angry or frightened. "Of course you would. I was an intruder."

"Then I… well, I wanted to keep your dirigible and everything aboard it." He looked away, and Arabella had the sense that he was about to admit to something she hadn't expected. "And you," he finally added.

For some stupid reason, that confession brought heat to her face as she remembered his tail wrapping around her in his hollowed-out mountain. Her pulse sped up. "I see," she said.

"It's a dragon instinct."

Just as quickly, her heartbeat returned to normal. Disappointment welled up in her. It was his dragon who wanted her, not him. She hated that she, ever the independent woman who would brave an Antarctic winter just to prove she could, craved his attention and affection. "I see," she said evenly.

If Xavier noticed her hurt, he didn't mention it. "I suppose I'll return to the university," he mused aloud. "If they'll have me."

"And what, get lost again?"

He shrugged. "Why not? Perhaps there's an Australian expedition coming up. There may be a place for me there, one with a better climate."

"There are people there."

"There's even more open space for a dragon to roam in peace. I doubt any venomous animals would affect me. I've been impervious to other poisons in other experiments."

"You experimented on yourself?" she asked incredulously.

"Naturally." He seemed affronted that she would ask, and she let the subject drop.

He was the one who changed it. "Why would your father's wife stoop to stealing your jewelry?"

The thought of Clarinda made her supper into a hard lump in her stomach. It killed her appetite. "She chases money. The authentic pieces I have are worth a considerable sum." Clarinda had asked about Arabella's selling the inherited jewelry at the wedding. "She's ashamed of me. She was ashamed of my father, too, and reworked him into her bastardized ideal of a gentleman."

Xavier hesitated. "Are you certain that you're not upset about your father remarrying?"

Arabella could have clocked him over the head for that remark. "No," she snapped. "If he had married someone who wasn't determined to meddle in the lives of everyone she meets, I would feel differently. If she accepted me and my father as we were and are, I would feel differently."

"Arabella…"

"I'm not a child. I'm not jealous that he remarried. On the contrary, I would have welcomed my father's wife if she acknowledged that I'm an adult and capable of making my own decisions. And mistakes, as you well know," she said.

"How does she meddle?"

Arabella bristled at the question. A dozen scenarios raced through her mind. Her focus on money. Clarinda's comments about her attire the first time they met: "You're far too delicate to be stomping about like a man in trousers and boots." Digs, subtle and overt, about her preference for living aboard a dirigible, even though Arabella's father had done so with her for years. Clarinda's ability to point out Arabella's spinsterhood every time she could, or remarks about her appearance. What was worse, Arabella's father had started nodding his head in agreement with his wife as of late. "It's *everything*," Arabella blurted. "There isn't anything on this planet that she doesn't already have an exhaustive and expert opinion on. Including my clothes, my dirigible, what I eat and drink, my interests, and my friends." Not that she had many in England, but she maintained regular correspondence with many of the people she met in her travels with letters and telegrams.

He remained silent.

85

"She never has a kind word for anyone," Arabella continued. "She's rude with the staff in shops and restaurants, she's rude to her own dinner guests. She's like a dog with a bone once she sets her target on you, nitpicking and making fun." The indignation she felt when the subject of Clarinda was brought up gave way to the familiar white-hot rage that consumed her when she had to be in the wretched woman's presence. She had to take a deep breath and remind herself that Clarinda was an ocean away. "And she feels entitled to my things. "My mother came from wealth and she left half of her estate to me when she passed away. I inherited it when I turned twenty-one. Clarinda resented that my father never took it from me before I could and that I wasn't willing to share it after she married him." How Arabella hated the obvious hints Clarinda dropped about how Arabella was wasting her money, that it could be better spent on improving her house in Torquay.

"She sounds dreadful," Xavier said.

"'Dreadful' is the kindest word I would use to describe her." Arabella ate another couple of mouthfuls of food, not wanting to discuss Clarinda any longer. She was in a beautiful city that she would soon have to leave, with company that she... well, strangely cared about. It was impossible not to, when they had saved each other's lives. "I told you about Clarinda," she said. "What deep, dark secret are you hiding?"

"Other than the obvious?" He gave her a wry smile, which made her heart do a maddening flip-flop. "Well, I nearly brought down the dirigible that brought me to Antarctica. I could have killed everyone on board while I arranged my disappearance."

Arabella stared at him, agog. "What?"

"I'd planned to fall off the deck about a mile or so

away from the coast," he explained. "To better prevent a search. No one would be able to conduct a marine search and rescue in the Southern Ocean. I was nervous and miscalculated the distance. I'm not as familiar with nautical terms and... well, it doesn't matter. The point is, I was supposed to have fallen in the water and shifted as I fell. Then I would wait in the water until the dirigible passed over me. But I fell in the snow instead, and the captain decided to try and rescue me."

Arabella's heart pounded so hard she was sure Xavier could hear it. If he could, he didn't let on. She hadn't known until then how badly she wanted to know his story.

"The dirigible crashed during the search. I was able to get away before anyone could find me and hid under snow in my dragon form. The other dirigible in the expedition saved the others. I don't know how many survived the crash, but I didn't find any human remains after I salvaged what I could," he said.

"That's why you were able to repair my dirigible's balloon."

He nodded. "I'm glad I saved what I did."

It took a few seconds for the weight of his words to impact Arabella. *I'm glad I saved what I did.* They sent her pulse fluttering again. "I thought you didn't want to return to England," she said when her voice returned.

Now it was Xavier's turn to look at the sun setting behind the railing, a small crease of worry between his eyebrows. When he spoke, his words were careful, measured. "Perhaps it isn't the destination, but the company." His amber eyes met hers.

There was an intensity in his gaze that made her shiver with anticipation for something she couldn't identify. She couldn't tell if he was waiting for a response. Not knowing what else to do, Arabella said, "Perhaps it is."

CHAPTER 10

The next few days passed without incident as they traveled. Xavier spent them belowdecks, giving Arabella some space in the flight box. He read Lucien Quinn's novel, one of his most recent books about a village gone mad, then read chapters aloud to Arabella after supper. She insisted that the village must be based on Gull's End, where the author holidayed in her family's ancestral home.

When Xavier thought about Gull's End, he thought of England and his imminent return.

He would have to rejoin society until he figured out a smooth way to leave it again. To rejoin society, he had to support himself. The only way he knew how to support himself and find a way to take off for parts unknown was to return to academic life. His prior expedition would find out about him, would want to know how he managed to survive so long on his own in the Antarctic. He weighed his options for lies and couldn't think of one that would be remotely plausible for someone with a lack of equipment to survive for as long as he had. He would have to be the

88

miracle that survived against all odds. He sighed as the realization hit him. He would possibly be subjected to attention.

Arabella called to him down the stairs from the flight box. "Xavier? We're due to land at the Vauxhall Airfield in about ten minutes. Would you like to see the view?"

He did not. Something in his gut twisted at the news, and it became much more real for him. He was truly returning to England. His dragon didn't care about where they were, though. He'd been nearly shouting at Xavier for the last three days, begging to be allowed out.

They were landing in London of all places. Where the hell would he be able to shift in privacy?

He climbed the stairs to find Arabella at the steering yoke, surprised to see the dour expression on her face. She wasn't happy to be returning, either. The sight nearly made him forget how the late afternoon sun picked up the fiery tones in her hair. "Why do we have to go to Vauxhall?" he asked. "You don't want to be here and I don't want to be here. Why don't you wire your flight plan to another airfield?"

"I have to check in. It's too late to change my flight plan now."

"So, we'll land, and then we'll head to another airfield." He paused, unsure how his next words would be received. "I have to shift soon. I can't do that in London."

Her hands froze over the yoke. "Fuck."

His anxiety about his impending shift was temporarily pushed aside by her use of the epithet. "I apologize for not telling you that earlier. I didn't even think about it myself. I'm so used to shifting whenever I need or want to."

"I understand," she said quickly. She bit her lip, a gesture that he shouldn't have found as charming as he did. "*Fuck*. All right, I have clearance to land at a few other airfields in England. I'll file another flight plan and we'll go there after we're docked here."

Surprise and gratitude kept him rooted in place. "Really?"

She looked at him like he had two heads. "Of course. Do you have a preference for where we should go? What do you need to shift here?"

He could have kissed her for her understanding. If he was certain she would be receptive to it and if she wasn't navigating a descent to Britain's busiest airfield, he would have. Now he was thinking about how much he wanted to kiss her. So was his dragon. It was uncomfortable.

She was waiting for an answer.

"I need open space," he replied. "Somewhere with as few people as possible." He thought about other ways it would be easier and more discreet to be shift. "Perhaps somewhere near water."

That earned a soft snort from her. "You're speaking about Gull's End, and I think Lucien Quinn wore out any welcome from Londoners that we might have had."

"You also said Gull's End's residents, as few as they are, are inexcusably nosy."

"I did, which is why going to that blasted house my idiot ancestors built is out of the question. I'm sure it's currently being rented by a tortured artist type, anyway."

The dirigible began its descent. Xavier felt himself starting to sweat. Not out of nervousness for who was at the helm. Arabella was a fine pilot, her crash into his mountain notwithstanding. This anxiety was for himself. He was truly rejoining society, if only for a little while.

The clouds gave way to a view of a familiar city, although with more enhancements than it had the last time he was here. New buildings had sprouted along the streets like mushrooms, smoke issuing from their chimneys.

Xavier could smell it from the flight box and his nostrils flared. He'd forgotten about London's stink and it would only get worse the lower they got to the ground. Gradually, people came into view beneath them, along with carriages, horses, and steam cabs. There were far more of the latter than Xavier remembered, likely of the hired variety.

The airfield itself appeared beneath them as the dirigible sailed over it. Empty wooden docks with gigantic painted numbers and letters drifted by until they reached the space for F-28. Airfield employees waited below them to tie the vessel down in place. Arabella expertly brought the dirigible to a gentle stop before lowering the anchor. The dirigible's descent sharpened and Xavier's stomach lurched in protest. He leaned against the flight box's glass wall for support. "Sorry," Arabella said. "That happens sometimes."

Xavier knew it did, had experienced it on long-ago flights, but he still didn't care for it. "It's no bother," he lied.

He didn't breathe a sigh of relief until the dirigible was anchored to the dock. Just as quickly, he remembered where he was, and it faded.

Xavier was back on English soil, once again out of his element.

～

ARABELLA STARED at the Vauxhall Airfield comptroller, trying to keep her temper in check. He seemed nice. He had sent her telegram to her father announcing her successful journey to and back from Antarctica without any fuss. The news he had just delivered wasn't his fault, and she wasn't about to proverbially shoot the messenger again the way she had when she made her Antarctic journey.

Every comptroller she spoke to along that trek had been correct about her lack of preparedness, after all but this new information was maddening. Not a single airfield in England outside of the major cities had an available dock immediately available for the next two nights, except for one. It was in the last place she wanted to be right now. "You're serious?" she said to comptroller in disbelief. "The only one with an immediate vacancy is in Torquay?" Where her father and Clarinda resided. Where Arabella vowed to avoid at all costs.

The comptroller pushed his spectacles up the bridge of his nose. They promptly slid back down. "I apologize for the inconvenience, Miss Greaves. However, according to the latest reports from our network, every dock at the smaller airfields have been accounted for. Torquay has one dock available for immediate occupation. If you want to rent it, I'll have to send the wire now. I'm sure it will be rented very soon."

"Whatever the hell for?" she snapped. "Who goes to Torquay when Spain or Italy is only a few hours away?"

"The weather is lovely this time of year."

Hadn't her father said that in his last letter to her? Why were there so many idiots who loved Torquay so much? What appeal did it have? The cliffs and endless seaside? Clarinda's ostentatious house left to her by her late first husband.

Cliffs. Water.

Open space.

Xavier might be able to pull off successfully shifting, if they made their way to Torquay. It wouldn't be as isolated as either of them preferred, but it was better than nothing. He would be able to fly off cliffs at night, maybe discreetly fly above the water. If nothing else, breathing flame over open water would be less of a fire hazard than if he did it above a city. "All right," she said. "I'll rent that dock. Could you wire the airfield, please?"

The comptroller let out a relieved breath, and she suspected he was waiting for her to tear into him. He turned to the telegraph machine at his side and typed a message to the airfield in Torquay.

Arabella fidgeted as they waited for a confirmation. She looked around the office, at the row of comptroller desks behind barred, glassless windows, telegraphs and typewriters at each employee's side. The space reeked of tobacco smoke and old food. It seemed like every surface was covered in a film. Cheap paperback novels and stacks of penny papers were crammed on wooden shelves, without any sense of organization. A rack of aviator gear that had seen better days was pushed against a wall, their price tags missing. It was a sharp contrast to the offices she checked in with in Havana or Charleston.

A reply came in a few moments later. The comptroller pushed the paper message through the barred window, across the desk. "Torquay's confirmed," he announced. "They're expecting you tonight."

"Thank you." She slipped the confirmation into her pocket.

Xavier was waiting for her on the deck when she returned. His mouth was set in a firm line, an anxious tic she'd noticed as of late. "I have good news and bad news."

He nodded. "Let's hear it."

"The bad news is almost every dock outside of London or Liverpool is occupied for the next couple of nights. The good news is I was able to rent the last one in a more remote area, and they are expecting us shortly."

He raised an eyebrow. "Why do I have the impression that there's more to this arrangement?"

"The airfield is in Torquay," she said quickly.

"I'd hardly call Torquay remote. Isn't your family there?"

"Yes, but I won't call on them. I sent a telegram to my father before I left the comptroller's office, letting him know I successfully made it to Antarctica and back. I didn't tell him I'll be in Torquay. He won't know I'm there," she said.

"Are you certain of that?"

"How else would he know? As far as he's concerned, I'm gallivanting around London with a drink in one hand and a handsome lad on the other."

A shadow crossed Xavier's face. He closed his eyes for a few seconds, as if in prayer. When he opened them again, his pupils had dilated in the way they did when he was in his dragon form. Something dark and possessive reflected back at her. Just as quickly, it was gone, and his amber eyes were back to normal.

A frisson of awareness zinged through her, overpowering the concern she should be feeling at his dragon-like eyes. She hadn't seen that look before, but a part of her liked it, dangerous as it was. It did mean he needed to shift sooner rather than later. "Let's go to Torquay," she said, damning the tremble in her voice. She tried to inject some normalcy, some levity into it.

While his eyes had gone back to normal, his expression was still shuttered. "Yes," Xavier agreed. "As soon as possible."

IT WAS early evening when the dirigible landed in Torquay, one of four other vessels in the entire airfield. The office was nothing more than a shack, staffed by a young man Arabella had seen during other trips to visit her father, but whose name she didn't know. He sat behind a rickety table loaded with the requisite telegraph and nothing else. The shack didn't even have so much as a newspaper rack.

"Miss Greaves," he said. His face lit up in recognition. "It's nice to see you again."

Xavier softly cleared his throat behind her. Arabella didn't bother to introduce them as she checked in.

"Where have you been?" he asked as she signed her landing confirmation slip. "You haven't been to Torquay in what feels like forever."

"I was last here in February," she replied curtly, and pushed the slip across the desk. "Which inn do you recommend? We're looking for a decent meal."

He looked surprised, then disappointed, when she didn't continue their conversation. "I suppose the Rose and Thorn. It's a short walk down the road, a red brick building with a big sign out front. You can't miss it."

"Thank you." That meant she wouldn't have to fuss around and find a vehicle to hire to take them to a restaurant. She doubted she or Xavier would be allowed in a restaurant in their current attire, anyway. In her experience, fine dining staff tended to look down on lady aviators dressed for the part.

As they walked away from the shack, Xavier said, "I think he's fond of you."

She shrugged. "I doubt he sees a lot of people in this part of the country."

"No, I mean the way he looked at you," he said. They turned on to the road that would take them to the airfield gate, and to the inn from there.

There was that fluttery feeling again. She thought she might know what he spoke of, but wanted to be sure. She *needed* to be sure. "What do you mean?"

"I mean, he doesn't have strictly platonic feelings for you."

Did that mean Xavier didn't, either? He'd alluded to as much, but he was speaking on behalf of his dragon. "Oh," she said. A nervous, humorless laugh escaped her. "Well, I don't know about that."

"I don't like how he looked at you."

That statement had her halting in place, a curious mix of intrigue and outrage welling up inside her. No one had ever been territorial over her, but she wasn't supposed to like it. "He can look at me any way he likes," she snapped. "I'm not a spoon to be hoarded under your mattress. *My* mattress, as a matter of fact." She almost regretted mentioning a mattress when she thought about it. It brought too many ideas to mind, ones that weren't exactly welcome at the moment.

Judging by the look on his face, he had thought of the same thing.

"I know this is caused by your dragon," she said quietly, mindful that they were on a public road. Even though there wasn't another soul she could see, she still wanted to keep Xavier's condition discreet. "But I'm a human. You can't decide that I belong to you." He looked like he wanted to argue, but just as quickly, his expression shifted. Arabella couldn't read it. Was it disappointment? Hurt?

"You're right," he agreed. "I can't. I apologize." He straightened his shoulders, as if in resolve. "I'm hungry. Let's get to that inn."

CHAPTER 11

*X*avier and Arabella shared a meal at the Rose and Thorn, their conversation more stilted than usual, at least in Xavier's estimation. Not that he had much to compare it to, given his lack of human contact over the last five years. He hadn't been the most social creature before his self-imposed exile, having spent most of his time in laboratories analyzing fossils.

Fossils. He hadn't thought of that word in a long time. Almost as long as it had been since he last set foot in England. He'd long ago lost that passion for them when he discovered that his physiology had so much in common with the dinosaurs whose remains he once searched out. Perhaps he had always known deep down what he was, long before he shifted against his will while in his fourth year of university. Not for the first time, he thanked the powers that be that it had happened while he was in his cheap student flat, alone for the holidays.

He'd long suspected something about him was different.

Maybe his parents had, too. He had never stopped

wishing that at least one of them could have survived their carriage accident, to tell him what he was and how to handle it. How to handle the compulsion to shift, to steal, to hoard. To keep Arabella Greaves with him. That was the worst compulsion of all, not the least because he didn't think she would share those feelings. Humans couldn't.

The memory of the Torquay airfield comptroller came rushing back, how the boy's face lit up when he saw Arabella. Xavier understood how he felt, what she looked like with windswept strands of hair dislodged from her braid, how her flight clothes fit. The confidence in her stride. He'd noticed that had returned since they left Antarctica and she wasn't getting herself in trouble again. The jealousy he'd felt was nearly overwhelming. It terrified him in its intensity. He hoped it abated once he'd had a chance to shift.

The sun had set when they left the restaurant, and they started the walk back to the airfield in awkward silence. Xavier hated it, hated how he managed to mess up everything when it came to Arabella. Or anything else in his life, really. "I'm sorry," he finally said.

"Whatever for?"

"For wrecking everything."

She sighed in exasperation and halted before turning to face him. "Xavier, what in God's name are you apologizing for now?" Before he could answer, she forged on. "We've already established that you have some unique challenges. You can't help them. Stop apologizing. I'd just appreciate some warning in advance before one of your attributes becomes an issue."

"I'm not fully aware of all of them."

"Haven't you ever felt possessive and jealous about other women?"

Having it stated so plainly brought a wave of heat

roiling through his body, a combination of want for her and embarrassment on his own behalf. He thought about Evelyn Putney, a fellow paleontologist from his days in academia. He hadn't felt the way he did about Arabella when it came to Evelyn. He knew she wouldn't let up if she suspected he was lying to her. "No."

His gaze met her shocked one.

"This is all new to me," he said. Frustration pulled at him, that he kept having to tell her that. "I have no idea what's normal for someone like me. That's one of the reasons I once wanted to contact the werewolves in Scotland. If a pack actually exists, they may know something about dragons."

"Why didn't you contact them five years ago? And why do you think werewolves might know about dragons?" She kept her voice low to match his tone, mindful of the occasional couple out for an evening walk.

"If a pack exists, it's reasonable to assume they've passed down their knowledge over the generations. I didn't contact them before because I wasn't sure who they could be, although I narrowed it down to a barony in the north. I can explain my theories to you in a less-public place."

"Back at the dirigible."

"Yes, back there." Thanks to hours spent in museum and university archives dating back hundreds of years, he'd pinned down the pack to a barony in Scotland. According to all accounts, they were hostile to visitors and ordered to remain where they were, unable to travel outside of their territory.

"I can't believe there are wolves anywhere in Britain," Arabella said.

"There aren't. There are wolf shifters in Britain. There's a very big difference. Shifters are still human."

"Yet you deny that part of yourself," she pointed out.

99

"You stay in the furthest parts of the world, away from everyone."

Indignation reared its ugly head, and he fought the urge to tell her off. "I do not deny my humanity," he replied stiffly. "It's because of my humanity that I prefer to keep myself cut off. It's safer for everyone. I'm sure the werewolves feel the same."

"You just told me that they were ordered to remain there, presumably by the government. I'm sure if they were allowed to do so, they would leave their territory from time to time. You have a lot more freedom than you think you do."

She was right, he realized. As far as he or anyone else knew, he was the only dragon in existence. No one knew of him, no one had placed restrictions on his movement. He had been totally free to travel to Antarctica and cause a potentially fatal dirigible crash to hide out in his mountain lair for years. He could have killed people because he was too frightened to seek out a werewolf pack and ask for their help in hiding in plain sight. Shame flooded him. It wasn't the first time, but it marked the first occasion it wasn't related to what he was. His own selfishness and shortsightedness came back to taunt him in full force. "We should find the werewolves," he said slowly.

"I like how you said 'we.'"

So did he. The thought of spending more time with Arabella had excitement thrumming through his veins, and his dragon wholeheartedly agreed with the notion. "But to do that, we'll have to return to London," he continued. "I don't have any of my notes from my research in the libraries. They were lost in the crash." He sighed. "I'll have to announce myself as a miracle survivor in the Antarctic to regain my university privileges if I want access to those books and files."

"Will that be so terrible?"

He bit back a harsh retort. By her own admission, she wasn't well-versed in academia's stifling social mores. "Yes."

"I can help you," she offered. "You aren't doing this alone anymore."

His indignation and dread gave way to a warm feeling in his chest that radiated through him. It was a balm to his soul, to know that he wasn't alone in this, if only for a little while. At some point, he and Arabella had to part ways, and he knew when they did he would be inconsolable. She would be the only thing he would miss about England. "Thank you," he finally replied. He wasn't sure how she would be able to aid in his research, but he appreciated the offer all the same. So did his dragon. It reminded him again of its feelings for her, excited at the prospect of spending more time with her, possibly in a university library. It would be a merge of his favorite things in the world: her and books.

It was funny how his dragon didn't react to the possibility of being around books again the same way it did about Arabella. Funny and frustrating.

They walked through the airfield gate as the sunset gave way to dark. The path along the docks was illuminated by electric lights on poles, casting shadows over the tightly packed cobblestones. Arabella's dirigible waited for them in the last dock at the path's end, a lantern blazing in the flight box. "Did you leave that turned on?" Xavier asked.

"Fuck," she muttered.

Alarm sprang through him. "Should we notify the comptroller? Does Torquay have a constabulary?"

"I would hardly call the child running that shack a comptroller, and I'm sure he's the reason that lantern is there." She grabbed his hand and started up the dock's stairs to the dirigible deck.

Xavier could have sworn that sparks flared between them at the touch, but he was too anxious to enjoy them. He followed her up the stairs, and just as quickly, she let him go. Damn it, his dragon *really* didn't like that. Xavier ignored it.

The flight box's exterior door was open and the hurricane lamp affixed to its ceiling brightly glowed. An angry sigh escaped Arabella as she strode through it.

"Wait," Xavier said. "Shouldn't we have a weapon? At least let me go below deck first."

"That won't be necessary. I know who's here." Down the stairs, she bellowed, "Father? Clarinda? Is that you?"

"It is," an unfamiliar female voice sang out.

Arabella's lips thinned in anger.

"I could have sworn that you locked this door before we left," Xavier murmured.

"I did. My father still has a key."

"There's still time for us to fashion a weapon from something," he said. "Just say the word, and I'll look for a tree branch or something."

That brought a small smile to her face. "I'll take care of them." Without another word, she climbed down the stairs, Xavier close behind her.

Crammed together on the sofa was a couple dressed in far better clothing than he had ever worn. A man vaguely resembling Arabella, his auburn hair streaked with silver, sat next to a dark-haired woman in her mid-fifties whose bustle and skirt looked to take up most of the piece of furniture. Her hair was perfectly coiffed in an elaborate knot at the side of her head in a style even Xavier could tell was a bit much for a social visit. Or break in, as it were.

"Why are you here?" Arabella demanded.

They both looked shocked, but whether it was at Arabella's question or Xavier's presence, he couldn't tell. "Am I not allowed to greet my daughter after a long journey?" her father said. He stood up and held out his arms.

Arabella pursed her lips and let him wrap her in a hug. "I made it to Antarctica," she said. "As you can see, I made it back."

"That was a foolish trip to take."

"I know!" Arabella snapped. Everyone in the room jumped a little. The woman—Clarinda, Xavier presumed—rose to her feet. "But I did it, contrary to the expectations of everyone around me."

"I don't see why you felt the need," Clarinda said, finally speaking. "A woman already completed that journey on her own three years ago. You weren't the first."

Silence descended over the dirigible. A muscle ticked in Arabella's jaw. A moment passed before she spoke. "That doesn't make it any less important to me," Arabella said, her voice low and measured. "One doesn't have to do something with the express intent of being the first." She took a deep, fortifying breath. "I'm surprised that you didn't begin with a hello, Clarinda. You're always so insistent on my following basic manners."

Clarinda actually looked offended. "It's rude to keep guests waiting."

"You aren't a guest, and I didn't invite you in." She sent a sharp glare to her father. "Why the hell did you just let yourself aboard? That's shockingly rude, even by my standards."

"Clarinda didn't want to wait outside in the heat," her father explained.

"What heat? It's not even sixty degrees outside!" Arabella protested.

"If you were dressed properly, you would feel the heat," Clarinda said.

"How did you know I was here, anyway?" Arabella demanded.

"Bradford told us," her father said. Arabella gave him a look that clearly questioned who he was, and he added, "He's the comptroller's assistant. He was watching the airfield today."

"Well, we're only here until tomorrow," said Arabella in frustration. She pointed at the stairs. "Please leave."

Hurt and irritation flashed across her father's face.

"Who is this?" Clarinda asked, tilting her head. Her dark eyes met Xavier's, and he turned away.

"A friend," Arabella replied.

"I presumed as such, but you only have one bedroom aboard this heap," Clarinda said.

"Oh, my God," Arabella muttered.

Xavier didn't have any experience with pushy parents, but he did with difficult academics. The only way to get them to leave was to give in a little. "Dr. Xavier Kinnon," he said, holding his hand out to her father.

Clarinda perked up when she heard his title.

"I'm a researcher at the Royal London University," he replied.

Just as quickly, Clarinda's expression shifted to one of disinterest.

"Jeremiah Greaves," Arabella's father said. "This is my wife, Clarinda."

"Have you any tea and biscuits, Arabella?" Clarinda murmured. "It's polite to offer."

"I would like to remind you again that it's even more polite not to break in to someone else's home." Arabella pointed to the stairs. "Leave. Now." To her father, she said, "I'll arrange a visit another time. It was rude of the comptroller's assistant to tell you about the comings and goings of tenants, not to mention how dangerous it is that an *assistant* was in charge of the airfield today. You know that just as well as I do. He's lucky if I don't send a telegram to the transportation authority for that."

"He's just a boy," Jeremiah said, but Arabella cut him off.

"Not now, Father." She pinched the bridge of her nose between two fingers, collecting herself. "Please don't do this. I'm entitled to my own space."

A resigned expression came over Jeremiah's face, and he nodded. "Clarinda, let's leave. Arabella, I will be holding you to your promise to visit."

She and Jeremiah shared another awkward hug, and Arabella stepped away before Clarinda could do likewise. She followed them out of the living quarters.

Xavier stayed where he was, wanting to give them privacy. He looked around the space, assessing it, but couldn't tell if Clarinda had snooped for Arabella's hidden jewelry, or any other signs of digging around. They hadn't helped themselves to tea or any of the biscuits Arabella picked up at the airfield in New York.

She stomped down the stairs a few minutes later, brows knit together in anger. She thrust a brass key at him. "You can keep this."

Xavier accepted it and turned it over in his hands. He knew what it was. "Why are you giving me a key to your dirigible?"

"Why do you think, Dr. Kinnon? My father can't be trusted to respect my privacy and autonomy."

His dragon urged him to hide the key away with the paste ring and spoon. Instead, Xavier slipped it in his pocket. Despite the circumstances under which he received it, he was touched that Arabella wanted him to have it. That she trusted him enough to keep it. Her use of his title in the mocking manner still rankled him, but he pushed it aside. She was angry, and rightfully so. It appeared that she hadn't been exaggerating about the difficult people her father and stepmother were, and he had to assume they were on their best behavior in front of a stranger. God only knew what they were like when Arabella was alone.

She rubbed her temples. "I'm sorry. I don't mean to be rude. I hope tonight didn't cause you or your dragon any more stress."

"I was more worried for you, actually."

She gave him a smile, the first he'd seen all evening. "I'll be fine. I always am. If I can take off from Antarctica with a fallen dragon on my deck, I can make it through anything." She paused, considering her words, before speaking again. "Well, you helped me take off, so I shouldn't take full credit. Oh, and Clarinda pretended to be concerned about your taking advantage of me and being after the family fortune, which is ridiculous since her primary motivation for marrying my father was his money." She sighed. "I need a drink. Do you want one?"

Before he could answer, she walked to the galley and removed a bottle of Scottish whiskey and a pair of glasses from the cabinet. Xavier realized he wanted a drink very much. "Yes, please."

She poured drinks for each of them and handed a glass to him.

"I can't believe I didn't notice this my first time here," he remarked, admiring the amber liquid. "Not that I indulged often when I was still at the university."

She clinked her glass against his in a makeshift toast. "Is it because of the dragon?"

He nodded.

"Do you ever want to tell me how you found out you were a dragon?"

He took a sip of whiskey and savored its pleasant burn as he considered the question. He wanted to tell her very badly. "Yes." He sat down on the sofa recently occupied by Jeremiah and Clarinda.

Arabella took a seat in the small chair opposite the sofa, a small table bolted to the deck between them.

He shook off his disappointment at not sitting next to her and began his story. It marked the first time he had ever spoken of it. He'd gone over it a million times in his head when he was still in Antarctica, lonelier than he thought possible. And yet, now that he had a chance to talk about it, he found himself at a loss for words.

Arabella didn't push. She took a sip of her whiskey and leaned back in her seat, waiting.

"My parents died in a carriage accident when I was young," he began. "I was only four, so I don't really remember them. There wasn't any family nearby, so I ended up in the care of neighbors for a few weeks, and then I was sent to an orphanage. I was adopted fairly quickly and was raised on a farm outside London. I realized early on that they adopted me for labor purposes and spent most of my time working on their farm. I learned to read while I was young, which helped my adopted parents, as their literacy skills were lacking. They sent me to a local school for a few years, but when I expressed an interest in attending university, they sent me away. I was sixteen."

He met Arabella's gaze, so sympathetic. She nodded.

"They didn't take well to my academic ambitions and were convinced I thought myself too good for their farm. I haven't seen them since and my letters to them were returned or unanswered when I came back to London. I enrolled in Royal London University, where I discovered that I have passions for paleontology and paleobotany I would have spent an uneventful academic career categorizing fossils until I got sick one evening."

"You shifted," Arabella deduced.

"I didn't. I was in my rented room one evening in my last year of my undergraduate degree and coughed smoke. Of course, that was terrifying, and then I coughed fire, which was worse." While he was used to it now, the taste had been horrific the first time it had happened. Xavier forged on. "The strange cough went away, but returned a few days later. I began shaking, and for a moment I thought I was having an epileptic seizure. Then I shifted. It was excruciating and terrifying. I didn't realize what happened until I caught my reflection in the window. I wished I could turn back into a human and I shifted back. I went to sleep, convinced I had gone mad, and then I found my shredded clothes on the floor in the morning."

"You shifted inside?" Her voice was incredulous. "I know how big you get when you're in your dragon form."

"I filled the entire room," he admitted. "I remember my tail was pressed against the far wall and my face nearly at the door. I don't think I could have turned around in there in that form."

"And so you just suppressed it until you went to Antarctica?"

"I tried to, and I took some trips out to remote locations so I could shift in relative peace. But it's never really safe to do so anywhere in Britain. There's always someone, somewhere, you know?"

She nodded.

"I continued my studies and took on a strong interest in mythology for obvious reasons. Hence my investigations into the werewolves in Scotland. That was obscure information, much of it in a form of English that isn't spoken anymore, but I found it. I only wish I had the foresight to keep a copy of my notes in a secure location somewhere in London. It would save so much time."

"Surely you remember some of the books?"

"I do, but there are still so many to dig through." The research wasn't the point of the story; he knew he could locate the information he needed more quickly this time around. "Because the werewolves were forced into staying in their territory, I had to assume there wouldn't be any leniency granted to shifters. Since I couldn't find evidence of any other dragons, I thought it would be best if I found somewhere to live out my days on my own. My shifting was getting more frequent and I was breathing fire more readily. I wasn't safe to be around others. "But I finished my doctorate first," he added. "That was important to me. I taught courses for a couple of years, too, just so I would have those memories to hang on to. I wanted to achieve my dreams for at least a little while. Then, five years ago, the Antarctic expedition was announced at the university and I managed to get a seat aboard it. My role was to look for evidence of prehistoric fauna and flora."

"In the snow?"

"It exists in the Arctic. Why not the Antarctic? Anyway, you already know my true purpose of tagging along to fake my death and spend the rest of my days in an uninhabited land. I accomplished that."

"Until I crashed into the side of your mountain."

Into the mountain and into his heart but he didn't say that, not wanting to make their friendship any more awkward. "Yes."

"Thank you for telling me." She regarded him thoughtfully under her sweep of dark lashes. "You've had a lonely go of it so far."

He knew that, but he still felt it as keenly as he did the day his parents died. He drained his glass, savoring its fire.

Arabella did likewise. "Want another?"

"One more," he said, before he could talk himself out of it. "Then I'm going to find a beach and shift."

CHAPTER 12

$\mathcal{A}$rabella had occasional opportunities to set foot at universities thanks to her travels with her father. She was usually bored as she was by anything academic, and spent her time lingering backstage of whatever auditorium he delivered a speech to about his lifestyle wandering the skies. She hadn't cared for the rigors of a higher institution of learning.

She wouldn't care now, if it wasn't for Xavier.

Something in his entire demeanor had shifted. There was a lightness to his step as they walked across Royal London University's campus, and he held his head a little higher. His back was straight, his shoulders squared. He made a quick visit to a barber for a quick haircut before they arrived at the campus, his first in over five years, and stopped in a shop for a new pair of spectacles. He looked like a professor, one who had returned home.

If Arabella had known that there were professors like him haunting universities, she might have applied herself a little more in her studies. As it was, she felt a little intimi-

111

dated as the gravity of who he was and what he had accomplished hit her.

He'd worked from the ground up to make something of himself. And what had she done? Literally coasted through life on a dirigible she maintained with an inheritance left to her by her mother. She had no other skills or hobbies, no passion for anything other than keeping her feet off the ground.

She was quiet as she kept up with Xavier as he strode through the building's corridors. He had sent a telegram to the university the night before, informing the administration of his miraculous rescue and his hope to return to academic life. A response hadn't been delivered to the Vauxhall Airfield where they were currently docked, but at nine in the morning, it was early by Arabella's standards. When she wasn't sailing, she was usually still asleep or just waking up at that hour.

It was yet another statement as to the differences in their stations and responsibilities in life.

They passed by what felt like dozens of identical doors until they reached the end of a corridor. Before Xavier could knock, it opened, revealing a man who looked to be in his late sixties. His white hair was slicked against his scalp, his matching moustache waxed. His eyes were wide and round beneath bushy white eyebrows as he took in Xavier's appearance. "My God," he breathed by way of greeting.

Xavier and Arabella stood before him, Arabella unsure what to do.

"Chancellor Grayson," Xavier said warmly. He held out his hand. "It's good to see you again."

He didn't notice it at first and stared at Xavier in disbelief. "It's really you," he said in wonder. "I thought the telegram was a cruel prank."

"I don't think I've made enough of an impact on the university's legacy to warrant that kind of foolery."

Xavier's practical, self-deprecating words seemed to snap the chancellor out of whatever daze he was stuck in. He shook his head a little, as if to clear it, and took Xavier's hand, pumping it up and down. "I am not a spiritual man, but this is nothing short of a miracle. Five years alone in the Antarctic. How does that happen?"

"For the reason you just stated." Xavier let go of his hand and touched Arabella's arm. An electric current of awareness sizzled through at the contact despite her leather flight coat separating them. "This is Miss Arabella Greaves. She's the aviator who rescued me. Miss Greaves, this is Chancellor Grayson."

The chancellor turned shocked eyes to Arabella. "You rescued him? Were you part of an expedition?"

She shook her head. "I traveled to Antarctica alone."

"That's a terrifying prospect." His eyes widened in surprise. "But I'm pleased to see you've returned in one piece and with Dr. Kinnon, too! How did you manage that?"

"The chancellor is interested in dirigible sailing," Xavier said quickly. "Or he was when I was part of the faculty."

"I still am, and I would love nothing more than to sit down and speak with Miss Greaves about her vessel," said the chancellor. "But right now, I want to hear everything about your time in Antarctica. The expedition was devastated at your loss. They will want to know of your return immediately."

"You haven't told them?"

"I wanted to be sure the telegram was genuine before I informed them of your return." His expression softened. "They grieved for you. They blamed themselves for your disappearance, even though by their accounts it was an accident." He tilted his head to the side quizzically. "It *was* an accident, correct?"

"Yes," replied Xavier quickly. "A horrifying one, but an accident nonetheless. There was nothing anyone in the expedition could have done to mitigate it."

"We'll sit down to have a talk about that at a later time," Grayson said. "Until then, the rest of the expedition members will want to speak with you. I'm sure you'll have a lot to discuss."

Xavier's smile faltered a little. "Yes, I'm certain we do. I also wanted to speak to you about the possibility of resuming my position. I know it's a great deal to ask, and I'll understand if that isn't possible given how long I've been away. Of course, someone would have already filled my previous role, but if there's a chance..."

The chancellor nodded. "I would have to consult the paleontology department, of course. There may be a place for you in our museum."

"Museum?" Xavier echoed faintly.

Arabella remembered what he said about museums and galleries, that a dragon couldn't be trusted around such treasures. Her heart thudded against her ribs as they waited for the chancellor's explanation.

"It's a new project," Grayson explained. "It isn't very large yet and it's very niche. It will focus on fossils and prehistoric plant life. I'm sure this would be a good fit for you, less difficult than immediately dealing with students."

Xavier visibly relaxed. "I think that's a good place for me to restart. I didn't have a chance to follow the changes in the field while I was away. I have a great deal to get caught up on."

"Dr. Putnam is leading the museum project," added Grayson.

Xavier paled. "Oh?"

She had never seen him react in such a way. Who was Dr. Putnam?

The chancellor continued on, heedless of Xavier's reaction. "Of course, I'll inform her at once that you've returned."

"Naturally," said Xavier.

Arabella was dying to ask about Dr. Putnam, but refrained from doing so. She was sure Xavier would tell her later, anyway.

"Shall I take you to the museum now?" Grayson asked. "I'll send word ahead of our arrival to lessen the shock. I'm certain she would love to see you again and know that you're safe."

"The visit won't be necessary," Xavier replied. "At least not immediately. If you want to let her know that I've returned, by all means, do so."

Grayson didn't pick up on Xavier's discomfort. "It's no bother at all. I can send a wire now and I'll hire a cab to take us to the museum site. It's only about a ten-minute drive away."

"I appreciate the offer, but…"

"Unless you traveled here in your dirigible?" Grayson said to Arabella. Before she could point out the obvious that there wasn't a landing site nearby, and that the sound of the engines would have drawn attention, he chuckled to himself. "Of course, you haven't."

She wasn't sure how to respond to that. "The Tube was sufficient."

Xavier had been a little nervous about that trip, she recalled but it quickly dissipated once he was aboard a train, something familiar he had done hundreds of times before he exiled himself.

"Let me have that wire sent," Grayson said. "Then we'll be in a steam cab and at the museum shortly."

Xavier sent a panicked look to Arabella when Grayson's back was turned and he retreated into his office, presumably to have his underling send a telegram. She tried to convey support in her look.

"What is it?" she whispered. "Why don't you want to go to the museum?"

"It's not the museum," he replied. "It's Dr. Putney. She was part of the expedition. I had no idea she had taken such an interest in paleontology."

"Is that why you look like you've just seen a ghost? Because another professor took an interest in dinosaur bones?"

"It's not the bones," he returned. "I have to tell you something. I…"

He was interrupted with Grayson's return, all smiles. "The wire's been sent. Brand new line, we've only recently installed telegraphs at all the campuses. You wouldn't believe the time they save."

"I would," said Xavier. "Shouldn't we wait for a reply?"

"Why would we do that?"

"Manners, I suppose." Xavier sighed in defeat.

"You didn't wait for a response before showing up this morning," Grayson pointed out. He gestured to the corridor. "Let's go."

NAUSEA ROILED in Xavier's stomach. If he didn't know any better, he might have thought he'd picked up something contagious on the Tube. He did know better, and he knew

116

the precise cause of his symptoms, and she was currently heading the university's fossil museum.

Unfortunately, Chancellor Grayson wouldn't stop chattering during the brief trip in the steam cab, eliminating any possibility of telling Arabella about Evelyn Putney.

A cynical part of him questioned why he was so anxious about their meeting. It wasn't as if he and Arabella had anything other than a perfectly platonic friendship, as much as that rankled his dragon. It was funny in a way that his dragon had never noticed Evelyn, or any woman other than Arabella. Funny and flummoxing. Would Arabella even care about his history with Evelyn? She had given no indications that she felt the way his dragon did about her. He now knew that it wasn't just his dragon that felt the way it did, it was him. He didn't know who was the influence on the other. With shaking hands, he helped Arabella out of the steam cab, every bit the gentleman he had never really been.

She wrapped her ungloved hand around his offered elbow, a gesture that offered him more support than her.

He needed the contact, would enjoy it while it lasted. He couldn't even take the time to admire the newly constructed museum. It was a one-story red brick structure, the front door braced on either side with large wooden pillars. Small figures of prehistoric animals and birds were carved into them, the skeletons inlaid with brass. The detail was remarkable, but Xavier couldn't bring himself to appreciate the artistry yet.

The door opened and a young, lanky man rushed out with his nose in a book, oblivious to the chancellor, Xavier, and Arabella. Xavier caught the door behind him and held it open for the others before stepping into a sunny foyer.

"What's wrong?" Arabella whispered.

"This is it," announced Grayson, looking around the

foyer in satisfaction. "The collection isn't as large as we'd like, but we've acquired many more specimens in the years you've been away."

"It's about Dr. Putnam," Xavier said, keeping his voice soft. "I don't know why I thought I needed to tell..." Bootheels tapped on the floor in a familiar cadence, one Xavier remembered well. It reminded him of rushing about the campus between classes, trying not to be late after he and his classmates had lingered too long over tea. He closed his eyes, as if to blot out what he had to face.

"Xavier."

He had never expected to hear her voice again. He opened his eyes to see Evelyn Putney standing in the foyer, as he knew she would be, a telegram in her hand. Her green eyes were wide with shock, her full lips open in surprise.

Her gaze never left him, even as she lost her grip on the telegram and it drifted to the polished floor. She took a few slow, careful steps toward him before reaching out. "Xavier," she repeated, drawing out each syllable. "You're really back."

Unsure what to say other than the obvious, he nodded. "How?"

"My friend, Miss Greaves," he said, glancing at Arabella. His heart sank when he saw the expression on her face, one of confusion and... hurt? That was impossible. "Miss Greaves is an aviator," he added uselessly.

Evelyn hardly spared Arabella a look. Her hand reached up to stroke his face, a gesture he guessed was supposed to be affectionate but he found unwelcome. He stood stiffly in place, not leaning into it. She didn't seem to care. "I missed you so much," she whispered.

Grayson cleared his throat and pointedly wandered down the corridor to one of the open doorways.

Before Xavier could slip away from her, she threw her arms around his neck and squeezed. Not knowing what else to do, Xavier briefly hugged her back, but just as quickly peeled her arms away from him.

Evelyn pulled back, clearly pained by the broken embrace.

"It's a very long story," Xavier said.

"We thought you were dead!"

"I know, and I apologize."

"How on earth did you survive?"

"As I said, it's a long story," Xavier replied. "A great deal of luck was involved. I owe my life to Miss Greaves."

Evelyn finally took notice of Arabella, her eyes scanning her flight jacket, trousers, and braided hair. It was a sharp contrast to her perfectly coiffed glossy dark chignon and blue dress, protected by a white linen apron. Evelyn had always had a knack for being put together no matter the circumstances. "Thank you," Evelyn said to her.

Arabella nodded.

"You must tell me all about it sometime," Evelyn said. Before Arabella could form a reply, Evelyn grabbed Xavier's arm. "Tell me everything," she said, her breath tickling his ear. She guided him down the corridor. "The rest of the expedition will want to know, too."

Arabella trailed behind them, stopping to pick up the forgotten telegram. When Xavier looked over his shoulder at her, he saw her expression was unreadable, something he had never seen from her before.

ARABELLA FOLLOWED XAVIER and Dr. Putney through the building, forcing herself to tear her gaze away from their interlocked arms. Instead, she tried to focus on her surroundings and what a disappointing museum it was. It only had two big rooms, for one. Fossils were displayed in glass cases, away from curious hands. There wasn't even so much as a reconstructed skeleton to be found.

I would've been irritated to have paid a fee to tour this place, she thought.

Although based on the lack of patrons, Arabella guessed this wasn't the sort of facility to compete with the South Kensington Museum. But she had to admit that the South Kensington Museum held little appeal for her, too, aside from displays about aviation. Her distraction was short-lived, as Dr. Putney steered Xavier into a room at the end of the corridor. A sign next to it proclaimed it to be for authorized staff only. Before the door could slam in her face, Xavier reached for it and held it open.

Dr. Putney blinked, as if she'd forgotten Arabella was there. Perhaps she had. Dr. Putney wiped tears from her eyes and gestured to the room. "This is it," she said. "I know you were so eager to see this happen."

"If you'll remember, I'd taken an interest in mythology before the expedition."

"But that wasn't your life's work." She picked up a small brush and dusted it over what looked like a rock to Arabella's unsophisticated gaze. She held it out to Xavier, who looked at with... was it disinterest? Arabella was unsure.

He held it for a moment and turned it over in his hands. "I didn't know you would take such an interest in fossils yourself. You were more interested in flora. If memory serves me, you were looking forward to harvesting and analyzing liverwort in Antarctica."

What the hell was liverwort? Arabella remained silent.

"I changed my focus after the expedition," Dr. Putney

replied. "In fact, I argued that the museum should be named in your honor."

Xavier looked mortified at the suggestion. "Dear God, no."

"The university said they didn't think they would be able to do such a thing for someone who hadn't even discovered a new species," Dr. Putney said in indignation. "Can you believe that?"

"Yes," Xavier deadpanned.

Arabella tried not to smile at his tone.

"I wouldn't want a museum named after me," he added.

"We thought you were dead and wouldn't mind."

Arabella would have laughed at that and the resulting look on Xavier's face, if Dr. Putney didn't look like she was on the verge of sobbing. Or throwing herself into Xavier's arms in a familiar way. The memory of it rankled her, an unfamiliar and immediately detested feeling. Arabella hated the jealousy that twanged through her like a string plucked on an out-of-tune violin.

"I would have," said Xavier. He looked around the room, but Arabella didn't think he was looking at the tables covered in dust and rocks, brushes and drop cloths. "I've never looked for that sort of attention. In fact." He cleared his throat and adjusted his spectacles. "While I look forward to working here if the university will have me, I intend to continue my studies into mythology and folklore."

Dr. Putney stared at him as if he had gone mad. "Whatever for?"

"It's an academic interest of mine."

"Are you going to start reading novels and poetry next?"

"I already do."

Dr. Putney gave him a look that clearly questioned his sanity. For once, Arabella could understand how she felt. The man had voluntarily hidden himself away at the South Pole for years and enjoyed fiction.

"Evelyn, I must be going," Xavier said.

"But you've only just arrived!"

"I didn't wish for a big fuss to be made over my return, as I told the chancellor."

As if on cue, Grayson's laughter could be heard from the next room.

Arabella didn't think Dr. Putney could look any more dismayed, but she was proven wrong. "There will always be a place for you here." She grabbed his hands, her consternation replaced by urgency. "Tell me you'll come to my sister's townhouse tonight. I'm already hosting the rest of the expedition survivors and some other university colleagues, anyway. I'd love it if you came."

For the first time since meeting her, irritation flashed across Xavier's face, only for a couple of seconds. If Dr. Putney noticed it, she didn't let on. "I've already told you that I didn't want to make a fuss about my return. I have a great deal to get used to as I reenter society."

"It's only a small gathering, and everyone will be so eager to see you and make sure you're really here."

"Evelyn…"

"*Please.*" Her voice had taken on a beseeching note. "I really need to get caught up with you. We left a lot of things unresolved between us, and I never dreamed I would get the chance to make things right again."

Nausea roiled through Arabella, and she briefly closed her eyes and took a quick, shallow breath to hold it at bay. Her thoughts tumbled around one another, each clamoring for her attention.

I have no right to be jealous.

He had a life and friends before I crashed into his mountain.

He didn't even want to come back to England with me.

He's never indicated that he viewed me as anything more than a friend but his dragon *sees me as more than a friend.*

Xavier Kinnon was more than his dragon. He'd tamed it, forced it to heel, and continued to live a life dominated by logic and reason. He led a life led by education, too. Arabella wouldn't be able to hold a candle to someone of Dr. Evelyn Putney's intellectual caliber.

"All right," Xavier said wearily.

Arabella and Dr. Putney looked at him with surprise. Dr. Putney's expression quickly shifted to one of delight. "Wonderful!" she said, all traces of her misery evaporated. "I'll be expecting you at eight."

"And you said this is a quiet, casual soiree?"

Dr. Putney hesitated for half a second. "Of course."

"I'm holding you to that," Xavier said. "And I insist Miss Greaves accompany me."

Dr. Putney looked at Arabella and blinked, as if remembering she was present.

She tried not to fidget, or compare herself to the put-together scientist. She rarely felt out of place in her aviator's ensemble and tangled hair, but today she did.

Dr. Putney pasted a smile on her face. "I understand. Of course, you're welcome as well, Miss Greaves. My sister does have a dress code for these events." To Xavier, she said, "It's unchanged from the last time you visited."

"You said this was a small gathering."

"I did, but I also said it's in my sister's home, and she insists on dress codes being followed," Dr. Putney explained.

"God damn it," muttered Xavier.

Dr. Putney looked shocked at the epithet, but didn't

mention it. "I'll see you both at eight. My sister's address is the same. It's still in Hanover Square."

"We will be there at eight," Xavier promised. To Arabella, he said, "Best we go. We'll need evening clothes for our visit tonight."

While Arabella could think of few places that sounded worse than visiting with Dr. Putney—chief among them visiting with her father and his wife—at least Xavier would be there. He'd stood up for her, insisted she be acknowledged. That had to count for something, couldn't it? She nodded. "Yes." She had an evening gown in her closet that would be suitable. Even though she preferred her more casual attire, she was still capable of looking like a lady when the situation called for it.

Xavier still needed appropriate clothes. Judging from his tight-lipped expression, he needed to get a few things off his chest, as well.

She walked alongside him as they left the museum, neither of them speaking. He ducked his head into one of the exhibition rooms to say goodbye to the chancellor, who seemed surprised to see he was leaving so quickly. He didn't speak until they were clear of the museum, back in the street. "Evelyn was part of the expedition," he said. "As I'm sure you've already gathered."

Arabella gave him the barest of nods.

"We had a personal relationship," he continued after a moment. He paused to look at a lamppost as if it was the most fascinating thing in the world.

"I assumed as such."

"It was complicated."

"I don't need the details." She wanted to know them, in a morbid way. Even though she suspected the knowledge might rip her heart out, weird as that notion was.

He shook his head. "We considered marriage at one point."

Arabella hadn't been expecting that. "What?" Sympathy welled in her at the thought of Dr. Putney being without her fiancé for so long. "You never told me you were engaged!"

"We weren't," he said. "The subject only came up. We weren't formally courting."

Color touched his cheeks at his implication. She never would have expected such behavior from him. Her sympathy gave way to indignation. "I never took you for a cad."

"I wasn't," he protested. "Her family wouldn't have approved of me. The sister we'll be visiting tonight is a viscountess. That was the sort of family Evelyn was expected to marry into."

"Her family approved of her paleontology work, yet are traditional and stuffy enough to expect her to marry into nobility?"

"She's already a noble," Xavier explained patiently. "Her father is a duke. Evelyn became engaged to a man of her standing shortly before the expedition. I found out two days before we set sail. If I didn't have my... shifting condition to deal with, I would have withdrawn from it."

Arabella's nausea returned. It wasn't just his dragon that compelled him to leave, it was a broken heart.

"Although it looks like she hasn't married at all, if she's still Dr. Putney," Xavier commented.

She couldn't reply for the lump in her throat. She blinked back unwanted tears. She hated crying, hated it even more with other people around. When she regained her voice, she injected what she hoped was levity into it. "You have a chance for a new start now."

CHAPTER 13

A quick trip to a secondhand shop had Xavier outfitted in his first evening wear in five years. The material was stiff and uncomfortable, an unwelcome change from his soft, threadbare attire in Antarctica.

Or going nude. He missed that, too.

His irritation over wearing formalwear disappeared when he looked at Arabella, who had transformed herself.

Her navy-blue linen and silk gown was simple, unadorned except for lace around the neckline that dipped lower than he would have expected from her. Her red hair was swept up off her neck, held in place with a paste jeweled comb of her mother's. Her hands and arms were hidden by a pair of matching navy gloves. She looked absolutely stunning but she had a guarded expression on her face as she stared at Evelyn's sister's Hanover Square townhouse.

Electric lights glowed in the windows and on lampposts on either side of the heavy black-painted front door. Beyond the gated garden, potted flowers in a riot of colors rested every few feet along the old-fashioned, perfectly maintained cobblestone walkway.

Already, Xavier could see people in the windows. Too many people for a casual evening spent in the parlor. Irritation and anxiety rose in him like a tidal wave, and he took Arabella's elbow. "We're not going in," he said.

Was that relief on her face? "Are you certain?"

"Very." Before he could explain that they had been duped, the front door opened. A liveried butler nodded at them and waited.

Just as quickly, Evelyn appeared in the doorway, a brilliant smile on her face. "Xavier!"

He suspected that had she not been bound by the propriety her sister and brother-in-law insisted upon, that Evelyn would have dashed down the front steps and walkway to throw herself into his arms.

She didn't run to him, but she didn't wait for Xavier and Arabella to make their way to the door themselves. Heedless of Arabella's presence, Evelyn grabbed Xavier's hands to squeeze in her own gloved ones. "I'm so pleased you're here."

"And Arabella," Xavier quickly said.

Evelyn's smile faltered a little. "Of course. Miss Greaves, thank you for coming."

Well, there was no way out of this now. With a sinking heart, Xavier followed Evelyn inside, Arabella lingering a step behind. As he suspected, when they entered the house, he found it teeming with people. Back in his Antarctic hideaway, he used to occasionally consider how he would react if he ever reentered society. If he would panic, or get anxious, or, God forbid, his dragon came out. As he stood in the parlor, a dozen faces around him peppering him with questions, all he felt was exasperation at being expected to talk with them. Then anger, when he thought about Evelyn lying to him.

He leaned over and whispered in her ear, "This wasn't what you said to expect."

Something in his tone had her eyes wide, hurt reflected there. "I didn't think you would come otherwise."

"You're right. I wouldn't have."

"But you're here now. At least spend a few minutes assuring everyone that you're not a ghost," she said.

From his other side, Arabella gave a soft snort.

No, he was something much worse than a ghost. In a way, Evelyn was correct, although he could never admit it to her. He had scared off at least a decade of the expedition members' lives when he disappeared. They deserved to know how he'd managed to survive all that time in Antarctica, and he could make up a few stories to keep them off his back for a little while longer. He gritted his teeth and faced the crush of people. "I wasn't expecting such a crowd," he said. He counted nineteen people, seven of which he went with to Antarctica, and another eight he recognized from his days in the university faculty.

Evelyn's sister, Juliet and her husband, Daniel, Viscount Renforth, waited at the far end of the room for Xavier to speak. Neither looked delighted to see him, or they could just be disapproving of the adoring looks Evelyn kept sending his way.

Xavier had no idea why she kept doing that, either. She was the one who broke it off between them in the worst way possible. He steeled himself, then started off his tall tale with the least-unbelievable lie he could think of. "While I fell off the dirigible, I obviously managed to survive, and made do in a cave for a few years…"

128

THIS EVENING WAS TORTURE.

Arabella wondered if she was in hell or maybe purgatory, but suspected that either would be much less boring. No one except Xavier ever paid any attention to her, and Dr. Putney whisked him away as soon as he had finished telling his dramatic tale of living in the Antarctic wilds for years. Perhaps it was for the best that no one noticed a nobody aviator at a party full of academics and aristocrats. While Arabella's family had aristocratic connections, she hadn't grown up in this world. She was barely acquainted with it.

And this *house*.

Its decorating scheme was so over-the-top that it bordered on gauche. Everything was gold or gold-colored, the carpets were so thick her heels sank into them and made her wobble. Renforth and his wife looked like they hadn't smiled a day in their lives. They wandered the room, speaking to select people while pretending their other guests didn't exist.

Naturally, Arabella went unnoticed by the viscount and his wife. It was just as well, since she had no idea what to speak about with aristocrats. Lonely and dejected, she scanned the room for Xavier and Dr. Putney and came up short. So, she looked for the next best thing: a liveried servant holding a tray of glasses. Some wine sounded good at the moment, if not half a bottle. She found the servant, who gave her a glass with the barest of nods. Even his uniform had gold thread in it.

"I've not seen you at Renforth's before."

The voice was unfamiliar, masculine and deep. She looked up at a man who stood at least a head taller than her, his curly dark hair clipped short. His nose was at an angle, as if he'd been in a fight or two. His dark eyes regarding her with more than simple curiosity.

Beneath his face was the body of a pugilist, albeit one wearing clothes that probably cost half as much as Arabella's dirigible's winterization. If she hadn't been pining for Xavier, she would have found him attractive. "This is my first time here," she said. "I'm Arabella Greaves." Was this how she was supposed to introduce herself to an aristocrat? She couldn't remember, but likely not.

"I know," he replied. "I was here when Dr. Kinnon told us his amazing story of survival in the wild."

"Oh, yes." She'd forgotten about that already, as had most of the other guests. Every time Xavier tried to talk about Arabella, Dr. Putney would interrupt and steer the conversation back to him.

"I'm John Bellingham."

Was she supposed to hold out her hand? Just to be sure, Arabella did. He surprised her when he took it and kissed the back of it through her glove.

"Dr. Kinnon mentioned you're an aviator."

At least this was a subject she was familiar with. "I am. Do you sail?"

"When I can."

"Were you part of the Antarctic expedition?"

"Hell no," he replied. "I'm a solicitor, one of Evelyn's cousins. Once in a while, I board a dirigible and the pilot lets me pretend I'm actually sailing it, but that's the extent of my flight expertise. I'm more interested in the vessels themselves. Dr. Kinnon said you traveled alone from Santiago to Antarctica. How did you do it?"

He looked genuinely interested, and Arabella was grateful for the distraction over her aching heart. She tried not to dwell on his being Dr. Putney's cousin and resisted the urge to ask him about her relationship with Xavier. Instead, she told him about winterizing her dirigible and the upgrades she'd made to it to withstand the journey. She felt herself start to relax a little, but whether it was from the wine or the conversation, she couldn't tell.

"How long will you be in London?" John asked.

"I'm not sure."

"I'll have to give you my contact details before your next journey. I'd love to see your dirigible and how you've kitted it out before you next set sail," he said.

There was a note of promise in his voice that hinted at his interest in something other than her dirigible. A few months ago, Arabella would have taken up such an opportunity, had some fun with him, and moved on. She'd done it before but that was before she crashed into a dragon's mountain. That dragon had disappeared from the party, as had the hostess, and the dragon didn't intend to stay in her life. Arabella forced herself to smile. "Perhaps in the future," she said, keeping her answer ambiguous.

"The far future."

A shiver raced down her spine at Xavier's voice behind her, and she whirled around to face him. His expression was unlike any she had seen him wear before: stormy, almost angry. She wondered what had happened with Dr. Putney while he was gone.

"I have to speak with Arabella," Xavier said to John. Without waiting for a response from either of them, he grabbed her elbow and guided her away from the room, through a set of open French doors that led to the back garden.

"Xavier?" He was acting odd, and she knew she should be outraged by his impropriety and possession, but she wasn't. Anticipation wound itself in her, coiled tightly, about to spring. She wondered what his plans were.

He didn't stop walking until they reached the far edge of the garden, a spot against the fence, hidden by a row of bright pink hollyhocks. Light from the house and a few gas lanterns strung around the garden bathed everything in a soft glow. He let her go, then faced her.

"Xavier?" His expression was unreadable, but Arabella needed to know why he was behaving as he was. "What's wrong?"

He ran a hand through his hair. He considered his words for a few seconds before he hoarsely whispered, "I didn't like him talking to you."

"John? What's wrong with him?"

"I just—I didn't like it."

Part of her was thrilled in a perverse way that he was jealous. The other was angry. "You've just spent the evening with Dr. Putney. I hardly think that places you in a position to judge me for speaking with someone at a party." Her ire rose. "A party where I know no one, and you took off!"

"I spent most of my time with Evelyn trying to get away."

"How hard could it be?"

"More difficult than one would expect. She cried, she apologized, she..." He sighed. "It doesn't matter."

"It does, if you're going to haul me away from a conversation with the only person who's deigned to speak with me tonight."

"Oh, my God." Xavier pinched the bridge of his nose between his fingers, clearly gathering his composure. "Her engagement fell through after I disappeared. I was her second choice, and now that I've returned, she wanted to pick up where we left off. Which was an argument, I should point out. So, we argued some more, and she is simply aghast that I have no interest in marrying into her family."

"Why not? She would be a good match for you."

"She would not."

"You're both scientists."

"I'm also a dragon," he whispered. "Have you forgotten that? And there are other reasons just as important that keep me from picking up what we had."

"You still had no right to drag me away from a pleasant chat about winterized dirigibles."

"It was *not* a conversation about dirigibles," Xavier said hotly. "As you well know. I heard every word of your conversation as soon as I reentered the parlor. I didn't like how *John* looked at you." Contempt dripped from his voice as he spoke the name. "I didn't like what he was implying. I can't stand him."

There was that curious, fluttery feeling in her belly again. "Do you know him?"

"I don't have to know someone to know that I can't stand him."

"You do, actually." Now it was Arabella's turn to be frustrated. "Why are you acting like this?"

"You know why."

"Is it your dragon?" A fleeting memory of his tail grabbing her flashed in her mind. His dragon wanted her, saw her as his.

"No, it's not only the dragon."

Before she could respond to that, Xavier took her face in his hands, and in a swift movement that took her breath away, kissed her.

CHAPTER 14

$\mathcal{X}$avier half-expected Arabella to push him away or slap him, but she didn't. Instead, she melted into his embrace, returning his kiss with enthusiastic measure. He moved his hands to her hips, the fabric of her dress bunching up beneath them as he tried to get closer to her through their layers of clothing. He felt like he was on fire.

His dragon snarled within him, urging him to run away with her like so much treasure to hoard, but he tried to ignore it.

Fury and jealousy rose in him like high tide when he thought about that bastard John talking to her about touring her dirigible. Arabella was *his*, God damn it all, and if he thought he could do so without scandalizing or ruining her forever, he would show that to every party guest tonight. His spectacles skewed off his nose and he reluctantly pulled away to straighten them. He could hardly catch his breath.

Arabella looked as he felt, spots of color high in her cheeks and breathing heavily. She stared at him, dazed,

134

and raised her fingers to her lips, as if making sure what had just happened, happened.

"Arabella," he said. She surprised him when she launched herself at him, mouth meeting his in a clash of lips and tongues. He could have sworn energy came alive and sizzled between them, as dangerous and electric as a live wire. Deep within him, his dragon commanded him to pull at her clothes, remove every cloth barrier between them and claim her in the viscount's back garden, propriety be damned.

He told his dragon to shut up, albeit reluctantly.

His roved his hands over her body, leaning into her, until her back gently landed against the garden wall. The gesture pulled a breathy, excited sigh from her, and she twined her arms around his neck. His hands slid down her hip to her leg, pulling up a bunch of her skirts. He raised them a few inches, then broke away from her to read her expression.

Her eyes were half-lidded with desire and it felt like his were, too.

His touch drifted higher, the material of her stockings soft and delicate beneath his fingertips. It was yet another layer of fabric between them, and he hated it. He found her knee and raised it, pressing himself against her, his erection cradled against her hips, in a pale imitation of what he really wanted to do with her. With his free hand, he reached for her gown's low neckline and pulled at the lace, ready to tear the garment from her body.

She put her own gloved hand over his, holding him in place. "Not here," she whispered against his lips.

Frustration welled up in him, further agitating his dragon who urged him to claim her as his where they stood. His other hand stilled under her knee, gently stroking her skin under its stocking. She let out a breathy sigh. "Where?" he couldn't help but ask.

He felt her smile against his mouth. "Somewhere more private."

His heart thundered in his chest, so strong and loud that he was sure she could hear it. "Are you sure?"

"Why wouldn't I be?"

Because he was a monster who wouldn't stay in England with her. Because he had just marched her away from a human man who was likely perfectly nice, or at least not a shapeshifting creature of mythology who would be a better match for her in every way. Because the beast inside him knew that if they continued what they were doing, it would never let her go, and that wouldn't work for either of them. Xavier had spent his entire life doing everything he could to not inconvenience or hurt other people. And the very reason that he lived so cautiously was screaming at him to throw it all away for a night of passion with the woman his dragon claimed. "I want you," he said, his voice a ragged whisper. "You don't know how badly."

"Your dragon..."

"It's not just my dragon," he said. He let go of her leg, and her skirts drifted back into place. "It's me." He ran a hand through his hair to keep himself from touching her again.

Arabella straightened, then adjusted her skirts and tugged up her gown's neckline a little. "You know, ladies like to hear that sort of thing. We *want* to be wanted." She looped her arms around his neck and pulled his face to hers, feathering a light kiss against his lips that had every molecule in his body at attention. "Take me home."

Xavier didn't need to be convinced. He knew he was being selfish. He only hoped she would be able to forgive him when he eventually left England again forever. His sense of responsibility fled as he adjusted himself, his clothes, and his spectacles, then took her hand. He led her through the house and kept his head down, not wanting to speak to anyone as they threaded their way through the crowd to the front door.

Evelyn appeared in the foyer before he could open the door. "Where are you going?"

"We're leaving," Xavier said, unable to hide the roughness in his voice.

Evelyn looked to him and at Arabella, at her lips reddened by his kisses and the strands of hair that had fallen out of its pins. Her eyes were glassy, the pupils dilated by desire. Xavier thought she had never looked more beautiful. He had to have the same look on his face.

Understanding dawned on Evelyn's face, then hurt and anger.

"Don't leave yet," she wheedled.

Without bothering to reply, Xavier swung open the door and led Arabella into the night.

CHAPTER 15

*A*nticipation surged through Arabella's veins as Xavier helped her into the back of a steam cab he hailed once they reached the street. It was an older vehicle with an exterior driver's perch, its tin sides dented and stained with the soot found everywhere in London. Its window glass was foggy and cracked, its driver abrupt and surly. Arabella didn't care when he closed the door behind her and Xavier took his spot at the steering yoke outside. Xavier took a seat opposite her, their knees touching.

The cab jerked into motion, its chassis vibrating beneath them. Some steam leaked into the windows through the cracks, filling the passenger compartment with a coppery odor.

Arabella ignored the smell, only focusing on the relative privacy she now shared with Xavier. *He looks like he wants to devour me.* The thought popped into her mind when she took in the feral look on his face, a stark contrast to his gentleman's clothes. She reached up and took off his spectacles, folding back the arms. She tucked them away in her reticule. "So they won't get in the way. Why do dragons need glasses, anyway?"

"This particular dragon happens to be myopic."

"Can you still see without them?"

"For my purposes, yes." Through the light afforded to them from the street lamps, she could see his eyes darken. He leaned forward, hands on her thighs, and let them drift upward over ribcage and breasts. Her nipples pebbled under the linen, and he toyed with the lace around the neckline.

He'd been ready to rip her bodice to pieces in the garden. She nearly regretted not letting him do that. Perhaps he would when they returned to her dirigible.

As if he could read her mind, he let go of the lace. "I know," he murmured. "Not here." He kissed her, slow and deep, his tongue demanding entrance to her mouth.

She was only too happy to give it. One of his hands left her torso to return to her legs, pushing up a fistful of fabric to touch her stockinged thigh. Her breath left her as she remembered how he did that in the garden, how he'd pressed his impressive manhood against her in a promise of things to come.

Xavier's hand rose, disappearing under her skirt to tease the sensitive skin of her inner thigh. His gaze never left hers and he watched her expression as his hand toyed with the edges of her drawers. "May I?"

The simple question warred with the ragged note in his voice, the stark need on his face but she knew if she said no, he would stop. She didn't want him to stop. "Yes," she whispered.

He shifted further in his seat, closer to her, gently urging her knees apart with one of his own. His hand under her skirt drifted closer to her core, the light, gentle touch setting her senses on fire.

She already knew she wouldn't last long. She couldn't keep a small cry from escaping her when his fingers slid inside her, and he silenced her with a kiss. "I wish I could do more to you right now," he murmured against her lips. "With my mouth..."

Just the notion of that sent a shudder of pleasure racing through Arabella.

"With my cock..."

The crude word was unexpected, but still did *something* to her. His fingers dove into her, thrusting into her in a motion that made her realize that her fantasies of this were weak and uninspired compared to the real Xavier before her. "What else?" she asked in a breathy whisper.

He nipped her lower lip between his teeth. "I want to rip this dress off you."

She was amenable to that. "Then what?"

His thumb found the spot that waited for his attention the most. Her back involuntarily arched against the seat. Xavier took advantage of it, quickly dipping his free hand into her bodice and pinching a stiff nipple before smoothing the neckline's lace again. "More of that," he said. He pressed his forehead against hers, and his hand under her skirt increased its pressure and momentum. She couldn't keep herself from moaning.

"I want to fuck you and make you forget that every other man exists," he said hoarsely. "I want to keep you for myself and let the whole world know that you're mine."

His words had all the effect of kerosene being thrown on an already raging inferno. She climaxed against his hand, waves of pleasure slamming into her as her body stiffened. Xavier covered her mouth with his own to keep her cry from escaping, not releasing her until her orgasm was nothing more than aftershocks sparking through her body. She felt boneless and weak, and thought he might have to carry her out of the steam cab. That wasn't an unpleasant notion.

Xavier slowly withdrew his hand and replaced her skirts below her knees. "I thought that might stave off my appetite for a while," he said. "But I was wrong. Christ, that was something to see."

His voice was still rough with desire. A quick glance at his trousers by the light of the passing street lamps showed Arabella that he was still in need of relief. She reached for his knee, intending to slide his hand up his leg the way he did to her, but he put a hand over hers. "Not yet," he said. "I don't want this to be over before it starts, especially in a cab."

Bright lights flooded the passenger area, signaling their arrival at Vauxhall Airfield. The cab lurched to a stop, sending Arabella forward into Xavier's arms. She peeled herself off him and they quickly rearranged their clothes before the driver opened the door for them.

They had arrived and had a promising evening ahead of them.

Xavier's libido had all but vanished during his last years in Antarctica, blown away with its winds once he carved out a place for himself in a mountain. It had stirred when he found Arabella in her crashed dirigible and woke up when they spoke for the first time. Since then, it had turned into an ever-present companion, reminding him of his younger days when all he could think about was sex.

This was different.

When he thought about it now, all he could think of was sharing that experience with Arabella. His dragon reminded of it nearly constantly over the last few days, its

141

insistence rising to a fever pitch until he couldn't think of anything else. He had never experienced those feelings for anyone else, not even after he discovered he was a dragon.

The steam cab left them at the Vauxhall Airfield's gate. Hand in hand, he and Arabella quickly walked through the sprawling rows of docks, heedless of the people milling about their docks. A light haze of steam and smoke hung in the air, the grinding and knocking sounds of dirigibles taking flight and anchoring omnipresent. They were the sounds of modernity and progress, and for once, Xavier didn't mind or resent them.

He squeezed Arabella's hand and stole a glance at her. Her red hair was more mussed than ever, her cheeks flushed. She looked like a woman who had just been debauched and was looking forward to more. *Which is exactly what she is.* The thought of the possibilities ahead made walking that much more difficult. He had never wanted anyone the way he did now, and he thought he never would again. Arabella had already ruined him for anyone else and they still hadn't had sex yet. The memory of her orgasm on his fingers ran through his mind. He didn't think he would ever forget a second of it. He didn't think it was possible, but his cock grew harder.

Damn it, if this gets any worse I'm not going to make it to the dirigible.

Arabella's dirigible waited for them, its flight box directly beneath a tall, glowing electric lamp post that reached into the sky. When she unlocked the gate to her dock, he saw her hands were shaking, the keys jangling.

He understood. He felt the same way.

Once she managed the lock, she took his hand and led him up the dock stairs to the dirigible. She switched on a hurricane lamp that hung from the ceiling in the lounge and turned to face him. She slowly started working her left glove off her arm, unfastening the row of tiny buttons that marched down it. Her eyes never left his face.

It was such a small thing, but intimate. Part of him longed to rip them from her arms, but he had already vowed to destroy her dress. It would be rude to ruin the gloves, too. He thought about a nude Arabella, save for her gloves. Perhaps another time. Would there be another time if he planned to leave England? It was best not to think about that right now.

She slipped off her glove, tossing it aside, and started on the other. Once she had unfastened the buttons of the right, Xavier took the liberty of sliding it down her arm, past her hand and fingers.

He traced his fingertips along her skin, noting her sharp intake of breath and how goosebumps rose under his touch. Now that they were alone, he was unsure what to do next. His instinct was to push her against the chaise lounge and rip away both of their clothes. Then he wanted to rut her like the beast he was but this was reality. As much as he longed to take her roughly and quickly, to mark her so everyone knew she was his, he held himself in check. Like the interlude in the steam cab, he wanted this to be good for her, too. *Mark her?* He quickly mulled over his thoughts. *What the hell is that?* Did it matter, anyway? He supposed it didn't.

Sensing his hesitation, Arabella asked, "What's wrong?"

"Nothing," he replied. "I don't want to hurt you."

"Of course you wouldn't hurt me," she said. She closed the small distance between them and ran a finger along his jacket. "You promised me a lot of things in the cab. You seem to be a man of your word." She looked up at him through her fans of dark lashes. "You'll keep your word, won't you?"

That was all the encouragement Xavier needed. "Do you want this to happen in the bed or the sofa?"

"My bed. I've missed it."

Without missing a beat, Xavier picked her up, voluminous skirts draped over his hands. He carried her to the bedroom where he let her go. Tearing her dress off her would be easier if she was still standing. "I noticed you don't have any nightclothes in here," he remarked. He switched on a gas lamp.

"Did you go digging through my drawers? I don't have much."

"I noticed that, particularly the lack of nightclothes."

"I usually sleep naked."

Xavier suspected as much. "I did in the cave, too, and speaking of naked, I can't help but notice that neither of us are there yet." His lips crushed hers in a fierce kiss, pulling her body against his. "How much do you like this dress?"

"Not enough to discourage you from doing what you promised to in the cab."

Xavier didn't need any more encouragement. With shaking fingers, he reached for the navy-blue lace at her gown's neckline and tugged. The sound of tearing fabric filled the room, the lace and linen easily splitting under his strength, revealing her corset beneath. It was like unwrapping a Christmas gift. He pulled again, exposing her matching drawers and stockings, a better sight than he had ever dreamed of. But it still wasn't enough. He pushed down the dress's sleeves until it pooled on the floor. She stepped out of it, then slipped off her heeled shoes. She took a small step toward him, lips turned up in a coy smile.

"That's only one thing you've promised to do."

"It is. Get on the bed."

Her eyes widened at the command, but she obeyed, sitting primly.

"Move further back," he ordered.

She did so, draping her legs over the edge.

"Lay down."

Arabella did.

She looked indescribable, a delicacy to be savored and he intended to enjoy every taste of her. He hooked his thumbs in the waistband of her drawers. Before he could ask if he could remove them, Arabella was already pushing them down her hips, revealing her sex. He slid the garment down her legs and tossed it away, not caring where it landed, and took hold on her knee. Kneeling before the bed, he put her leg over his shoulder and ran his hands over her thighs to the tops of stockings. He'd already decided she would leave them on.

"Xavier," said Arabella, her voice a breathy whisper. She shivered with excitement, and one hand stroked his hair. "You promised."

That was all the encouragement he needed. He pressed his mouth against her, drawing a cry of pleasure from her. Her fingers tightened their grip on his hair, urging him on, and he was only too happy to comply. His tongue found the bundle of nerves that she guided his head to, and her body already started to shake and quiver beneath him. She was close to coming undone again, and he didn't think he would ever tire of seeing and feeling it.

Inside him, his dragon snarled to take her, spirit her away. He shushed it.

He pressed two fingers inside her and the motion was enough to send her over the edge again. He loved that she didn't try to be quiet, was so open with him, that she pulled at his hair. He loved how his name sounded when she came, how her thighs shook on either side of his head.

Once her cries had subsided, he gently nipped at the exposed skin above her stocking and rose to his feet. His cock was so hard it hurt, and he wasn't sure how long he could last. It had been so long, and he had never wanted anyone the way he did Arabella.

She levered herself up on her elbows to take him in, at his still-dressed state. With shaking fingers, he started work on his shirt buttons, then his trousers.

"Take off your corset," he commanded.

Arabella sat up, then deftly unhooked her corset. Slowly, she peeled the sides apart to reveal it was silk lined, that she wore nothing underneath, and set it aside.

Xavier's mouth went dry as he pushed his trousers and underclothes off his body, then shucked his shirt. Arabella watched him through heavy-lidded eyes, as he leaned over her and kissed her. It was sweet, almost gentle, a sharp contrast to the inferno of desire currently burning in him that told him to take her immediately. He threaded his fingers through hers and held her hands on either side of her head. His lips traced a line down her jaw, to her throat, her collarbones. He kissed the swell of her breast and sucked one pebbled nipple into his mouth.

Her hips bucked against his, and he let go of one of her hands to grasp her other breast, kneading and squeezing until she let out those breathy little moans again. "Xavier," she moaned. Her hand gripped his. "Please."

He let go of her nipple. "Please what?"

"Please keep your promise."

He raised his head and feathered a kiss at her pulse beating a rapid tattoo in her neck. She shivered. "Which part?"

"The part where you said you were going to fuck me until I forgot any other man existed."

The mention of other men, even though she quoted

him, had his dragon on edge again. The question reminded him of something else that he should have brought up already. "Have you done this before?"

She took another sharp breath, but he could tell this wasn't desire.

He hoped he hadn't just fucked up everything. "I don't want to hurt you," he quickly added. "If this is your first time, I want this to be good for you."

"It isn't," she replied. "I know what I'm doing. Will that be a problem?"

"Of course not." As long as there weren't any others.

"I'm certain you'll make this good for both of us," she said. She wriggled her hand out from his grip and laced her fingers around his neck, pulling him to her for a kiss.

He urged her knees apart and settled against her hips, taking himself in hand to push inside her. Both of them moaned, her body wriggling beneath him as she adjusted, his already quivering at her warmth. Slowly, he began to thrust, each one drawing a gasp from her. Her legs wrapped around him, pulling him deeper into her as his pace increased until he slammed into her body.

Her hips met his with each movement, his name on her lips.

He captured them with his own as her body began to shake in another climax and felt his building. It wouldn't be long. His gums itched for a moment, and he broke the kiss. Just as quickly, the sensation was gone, but the inside of his mouth felt strange. That feeling was fleeting, too. Instead, all he could focus on was Arabella's face as she looked in the throes of orgasm, an expression that hastened his own. He lowered his head again to her neck as his climax ripped through him, where her neck where it met her shoulder. The motion muffled his yell as his body shuddered inside her. As he pressed a kiss to the spot he'd bitten, soothing the hurt, he realized he'd made a mistake.

She had ruined him.

He would never be able to let her go.

ARABELLA SNUGGLED against Xavier's chest, unable to bring herself to move just yet. His arms tightened around her and he dropped a kiss to the top of her head, a comparatively chaste gesture compared to what they had just shared. Just the thought of what they had done brought heat to her face. She would treasure those memories for the rest of her life. "What happens next?" she murmured against his skin.

"You could give me back my spectacles. They're still in your reticule."

"So you'll be able to see me as I am?" she teased.

"I already have," Xavier said. He tilted her chin up to better look her in the eye. "You'll note I deliberately left the light on and I can see you just fine with myopia." He traced the back of his hand against her face, sending electric sparks dancing across her skin.

She sighed and leaned into him, not wanting to break the contact.

His hand dipped lower, down her neck to where it met her shoulder. He frowned as he reached the spot where he bit her.

"What is it?" Arabella touched it, finding a slightly raised spot. "You left quite the mark on me."

"Yes, I didn't intend to do that." A furrow of worry appeared between his brows.

"It's all right. No one's bitten me before. I can't say I didn't like it."

148

"Arabella…"

"No one's ever ripped off my clothes, either. I'd like to do that again."

His pupils dilated in the soft light, but his expression didn't change. "I think you should look at it," he said hoarsely. "In the looking glass."

There was an urgency to his tone and set off klaxons in her mind. She reluctantly got out of bed and padded on her stockinged feet to the small looking glass bolted to the wall. She pushed her hair aside to look at the bite. The mark was raised, two spots where his incisors sank into her skin. It already looked like it was healing. The wound didn't hurt when she gingerly touched her fingertips to it. "What did you do to me?" she said aloud. "Not that I'm complaining."

"I'm not either but I've never done that before."

"Well, it's been a few years, hasn't it?" She returned to the bed and nestled against his naked chest. "Perhaps you're simply out of practice and if that was you out of practice—" She lightly nipped his skin under his ear. "I'd really like to see how you do things under normal circumstances."

His arms tightened around her again. "I would be only too happy to show you," he said, his breath ruffling her hair.

Xavier's voice held a note of promise, and like the others he had made, Arabella would hold him to it.

CHAPTER 16

*S*pring sunshine flowed through the bedroom's lone porthole, a rare sight in London any time of year. Xavier rolled over to face Arabella, who slept peacefully next to him. Her breathing was deep and even, and he was loath to disturb her. He smiled to himself as he ran over the previous night's events in his mind. He reached out and touched her hair spread over the pillow, as if to make sure she was still real and still in his bed. Well, *her* bed, technically. Even though he had turned it into his makeshift treasure trove. The cutlery and jewelry he'd filched was still secured under the mattress.

Arabella shifted, revealing the bite mark he left on her. His blood ran cold.

It looked healed, like a scar she'd had for years. What was more, the mark didn't look like it could've been made by human teeth.

He searched the inside of his mouth with his tongue, trying to see if his incisors felt different. They didn't but they had itched last night in the throes of passion, hadn't they? He had a hazy recollection of that feeling. He'd been too preoccupied with what the rest of his body was doing at the time. He still had a distinct memory of feeling like his teeth were bigger, somehow.

Oh, Christ, what have I done to her?

Not for the first time, Xavier desperately wished there was another dragon shifter he could speak to. A mention of dragons in the archives he'd combed through like the ones he'd found about werewolves would have been helpful, too, if only marginally. *Why have I always had to be alone? Why couldn't my birth parents have stayed alive and told me stories about our ancestors?* Taking care not to disturb Arabella, Xavier slipped from bed and tiptoed to the looking glass. Inspecting his teeth, he found nothing amiss. What the hell had come over him last night? It wasn't just his teeth and the wound he'd left on Arabella. It was everything else. It had been years since he'd last been with a woman, but he didn't think that would account for the rest of his behavior. He wasn't usually so... demanding. Dominant.

The rustle of fabric behind him had him turning around to face a yawning Arabella. "Come back to bed."

He wanted to, more than anything but the pressing matter of finding out more about what he was pulled at him. "I'd planned on going to the university archives today to try and reconstruct my research."

She leaned back against the pillow and heaved a dramatic sigh. "I'm sure that could wait for a little while."

"I'd prefer to get there as soon as it opens."

"Is there such a demand for moldy old books that you have to get there before it gets busy?"

"You might be surprised."

"Ugh!" She pounded her fists into the bedclothes. "Fine. As long as I can go with you. It will be boring having nothing to do at the airfield."

"You might find it just as boring searching through piles of moldy old books, too."

She threw back the bedclothes and stood up.

Xavier swallowed and reconsidered his decision to leave the bedroom at all.

"I'd rather be with you and be bored," she said, surveying the room. She picked up the shredded remains of her navy-blue dress. "And I'm not implying that you're boring."

"No, I understand."

She tossed the pieces aside. "Who knows, I may actually be able to be of help today." She opened the wardrobe and pulled out a fresh set of flight clothes. "I'll be ready to leave in half an hour." Tossing the clothes on the unmade bed, she sighed. "I won't take long to wash up and make some tea."

"Go wash up," Xavier said. He reached for her, and she eagerly slipped into his arms. God damn it, she was really testing his resolve today.

He kissed her, relieved to find that the same sparks he'd felt the night before, if not since the first time he saw her, were still there. His dragon certainly seemed happier, at least.

"I'll make tea," he promised.

UNTIL THAT MORNING, Arabella would have been appalled at the suggestion that she spend an hour, let alone the entire day, at a library. A part of her was already bored at the prospect, but the rest was ecstatic at the idea of spending as much time as she could with Xavier. The need to stay with him, to keep in sight within grabbing range, was brand new to her. She'd never felt that way about any of her other lovers, preferring to maintain a polite distance out of the bedroom. It was a weird feeling, but also felt right in a way she never expected it to.

When she was dressed and her hair held back in its customary braid, she picked up the shredded remains of her dress from the floor. She felt her whole body blush as she held the ruined fabric and examined it, wondering if it could be fixed. The linen and silk was beyond repair. She folded it up and left it at the bottom of her closet.

She and Xavier shared a quick breakfast before they left the airfield, then headed for the university library. It was an unusually beautiful early summer day in London, the streets flooded with sunshine with nary a cloud to be seen.

Walking arm-in-arm with Xavier, Arabella realized she was happy for the first time in a long time. When was the last time she'd been content like this? She couldn't remember.

Xavier stopped in a shop to buy a notebook and pencils for his research, then hailed a steam cab. Once the driver closed the door behind them, Arabella felt herself blush when she looked at him sitting across from her.

As if he could read her mind, he said, "I suppose you're thinking about last night, too."

She nodded and couldn't keep herself from giggling like a schoolgirl.

Color touched Xavier's cheeks and he couldn't hide a smile, either. "I'm... I'm not usually like that," he confessed.

"Can you still be like that?" she asked, keeping her voice low. "For next time?"

He reached for her hands and threaded his fingers through hers. "I don't think I can't not be like that," he said. "What I feel for you is overwhelming. It's almost frightening."

Arabella's breath caught and a strange quiver took hold in her stomach. No one had ever confessed to such a thing with her, and she found it intriguing. There was something incredibly alluring about knowing that he felt so intensely for her. Not the least because she felt it, too. It was a feeling that had been steadily growing since he grabbed her with his tail in his Antarctic lair, what felt like a million years ago.

"I wonder what it means," Xavier continued, a thoughtful look crossing his face.

"I would presume it means you care about me."

He raised an eyebrow at her. "I mean, I haven't felt jealous or possessive over anyone until I met you. I was ready to tear apart that bastard John's limbs last night."

It took a few seconds for Arabella to remember who he was talking about. John Bellingham, she recalled. The man who wanted to see her dirigible and more. "We were only talking," she said.

"I know and even though I didn't care for the way he looked at you, I still shouldn't have dragged you away like I did. I apologize for that."

"You didn't," she protested. "And I should tell you that I spent the entire night up until the garden absolutely miserable."

"It was a miserable party we were tricked into attending." He squeezed her hands. "Although I must say you looked incredible."

She felt herself blush again, but forged on. "It wasn't just the party," she explained. "I was upset and hurt that you went off with Dr. Putney and spent the evening moping around the house. She's someone you have a history with and will probably see when you return to the university. I don't have the right to dictate who you spend time with. Neither of us do."

"Evelyn lied and manipulated me into a makeshift welcome home party," Xavier corrected. "Then she spent the better part of the night ignoring the rest of her guests while pleading with me to take up our relationship where it left off. She locked her study door at one point and I didn't want to break it down to get out. It took a while to convince her."

"Why the hell didn't you tell me this last night?"

There was that eyebrow again. "I was distracted. Her behavior was such that I don't want to pursue a position at the university museum under her leadership. I'm going to look for something else in another department."

"You don't have to work at all," Arabella said. "I'm financially secure and very responsible with money. We could sail the skies together and you could, I don't know, write about dinosaur fossils if you want."

Xavier leaned back against the scarred leather squabs.

Something in her seized and she wondered if she said the wrong thing but it was true. She did have a trust, one that her father and his wife couldn't access, and it was well-managed. She lived modestly for an aviator.

"I need to work," he said. "At least in some capacity. Do you think you would enjoy sailing to excavation sites? It isn't the most glamorous work and there's a great deal of sitting still and dusting big chunks of rock with a small brush, but…"

A thrill coursed through her and she nearly leapt on him from her seat. She put everything she could into her kiss, a promise of the future together, whatever that may hold.

He had changed his mind about leaving her. He responded immediately, but just as quickly as it started, he broke it. Arabella didn't move from his lap, instead keeping her gaze fixed on his face.

"I think I would like that," she said.

Any further conversation was halted when the steam cab lurched to a stop. Arabella looked out the vehicle's grimy side window. "I believe we've arrived."

They disentangled themselves from each other just before the driver opened the door to let them out. Arabella handed him a few coins for the fare, then took in the grand building ahead of them. Like she did at the university and Dr. Putney's home, she felt intimidated in front of it. It soared six stories high, its mullioned windows looking like dozens of judging eyes that silently rebuked her for her distaste of anything academic.

Xavier took her arm, snapping her out of her thoughts. "Let's go." He led her along the cobbled path to the building's entrance. The path was flanked by expanses of green lawn on either side, and trees that were in early bloom. A few people milled about; like the day before at the university museum, none wore flight clothes.

If they were going to make visiting universities and libraries a regular occurrence, Arabella thought she ought to invest in a proper day dress of some kind to blend in a little more but no one paid her or Xavier any mind as they walked through the door to a cavernous foyer. Sunlight flooded the space from a window in the ceiling six floors above them, and rows of tables were arranged in straight lines down the middle. Everywhere there were shelves of books. Balconies above their heads were crammed with them and people with their noses buried in them. What struck Arabella most was its eerie quiet. Dimly, she was aware of the bustle of London's streets outside but the noise took second place to the near-silence. She thought if she so much as whispered a question to Xavier, she would earn the collective wrath of everyone in the building.

Xavier purposefully guided her through the library, his arm still in hers. "Little has changed since I was last here," he whispered in her ear. "I don't think the patrons have moved, either."

That brought a smile to her face.

He walked to a large desk where a silver-haired woman stood behind.

She was one of only a few women wearing trousers, something that hadn't escaped Arabella's notice during their walk. The woman smiled, then did a double take. She leaned across the desk and hoarsely whispered, "Didn't you fall off a dirigible?"

Xavier gave her a tight half-smile. "I did, and I've returned."

She lowered her thick-lensed spectacles and squinted at him. "You're really Dr. Kinnon, back from the dead?"

"I'm really Dr. Kinnon, and I was never dead in the first place," he whispered.

She reached across the desk for his free hand. "Bless you," she said fiercely, voice just above a whisper. A tear slid down her cheek. "I may have to go to church again just to personally thank whoever's in the sky for your safe return." She let go of him to wipe her eyes.

"You don't have to do that on my account."

She sniffled. "I should probably check in with him or her or whoever, anyway. The mister will be very happy to hear of your return. What brings you here?"

He gestured to Arabella. "My companion and I will be continuing my previous research today. Arabella, this is Mrs. Greene, one of the librarians. We were friendly before the expedition."

She looked Arabella up and down. "Aviator?"

Arabella nodded.

"It's nice to hear of ladies at the yoke. Dr. Kinnon, you shall come to my home for supper one night soon to tell me and the mister all about your adventures." She nodded at Arabella. "Bring your companion. I like aviators almost as much as professors."

A library patron walking by the desk, a stack of books in his arms, looked at the silver-haired woman and deliberately coughed.

"Stop being a fusspot!" she hissed. To Xavier and Arabella, she said, "I believe I saved some of your notes."

The color drained from Xavier's face. "I beg your pardon?"

"You were doing research in the stacks on your last visit here," she repeated. "You left a notebook behind and never returned for it. I saved it."

Xavier stared at her, dumbfounded. When he found his voice, he said, "You've saved my notes all these years?"

"Of course I did." Mrs. Greene looked indignant at the very notion of tossing out someone else's possessions. "It was a memento of a friend who had passed who shared much of my interests. Let me look for it in my office. I'll return shortly." Without waiting for another word, she shuffled away, down a corridor behind the gigantic desk.

Xavier stared at her retreating figure. "How?" he breathed.

The same man who coughed in Mrs. Greene's direction passed by them again and whispered, "Will you *please* be quiet? People are trying to work."

Neither of them spoke until the librarian returned a few moments later, holding a small leather-bound notebook. She leaned over the desk and pressed it into Xavier's hands. "The lower stacks are quiet today," she said softly. "And I should tell you that some of the materials have been removed, by order of the government." She narrowed her eyes at someone over their shoulders, and Arabella guessed the shushing man was glowering at her. Mrs. Greens looked around her desktop for a few seconds, then found a sheet of foolscap and pencil. She wrote a note on it before folding it in quarters and handing it to Xavier.

Xavier accepted it without reading the note and nodded at Mrs. Greene in thanks, then led Arabella away from the desk.

Her curiosity had her longing to pull it out of his hand and read it herself. She remained quiet as he led her through the library and down a corridor. At the end of it, he opened a door to reveal a staircase lit with electric torches. She looked down. "What's here?"

"The lower stacks," he whispered.

So, *that's* what the term meant. She followed him down the stairs, pleasantly surprised to see the basement was well-lit without a trace of damp or cold. The masses of books and documents crammed on shelves, with only a couple of feet of space between them, muffled all sound. Arabella couldn't decide if the stacks were cozy or claustrophobic.

Xavier took her hand and led her down one of the tiny corridors between the shelves.

Claustrophobic, she decided. It was definitely claustrophobic. At the other end of the shelves was a row of open sliding doors that revealed tiny rooms. A small desk and chair was in each, bathed in light from electric torches on the walls. Flameless candles sat at each table for extra light.

Xavier picked one at random and switched on the flameless candles, then slid the door shut behind them.

It reminded Arabella of being in the belly of a dirigible when its power supply was shut off. That had happened once, when she was sailing with her father. It was a frightening but thankfully short-lived experience when she was twelve or thirteen years old. She remembered helping him adjust the vessel's helium flow to safely land it for repairs.

"What are you thinking about?" Xavier asked. He set the notebook and foolscap on the tabletop.

"Can we speak in here?"

"As long as we're quiet."

"Being down here reminded me of an incident aboard a dirigible when I was a child," she replied. "The engine and helium supply failed. My father and I had to rearrange things to make a safe emergency landing. This is what the engine room aboard that dirigible felt like."

His eyes widened in concern. "Would you prefer that we leave?"

"No, I'll be fine. I just hadn't thought about that incident in years." She looked at the closed door. "Has one of the shelves ever fallen?"

He smiled. "Not to my knowledge."

"I suppose no one would hear it, anyway." She looked at the folded note, her curiosity getting the better of her. "What does it say?"

He sat down in the lone chair, then pulled her into his lap. He unfolded the foolscap and both silently read the words written in a looping scrawl:

Agents of H.M.'s government arrived in the spring of last year to remove materials you took your mythology research from. The catalogued books and documents taken pertained to wolves, which I remember was part of your interests, as well as some other documents relating to geography. I apologize for their loss, Dr. Kinnon.

Xavier pushed the note away. "The government knows," he whispered.

Arabella picked up the desperate note in his voice and twisted around to face him. "But not about you," she replied. Even though they were alone, she kept her voice low. "You told me you found evidence of a werewolf group somewhere in Scotland. Would it be impossible for the government to know of them, too? Perhaps they were protecting them."

"Or protecting others from them or experimenting on them. There's no end to the possibilities that could have befallen them."

"If they were vicious, wouldn't they have already attacked humans?"

Xavier considered her words. "We wouldn't hear about it if the powers that be didn't want us to."

Arabella tried to look at the positives of the situation. "This means that the wolves exist," she said. "Now, it's simply a matter of discovering where they could be. Mrs. Greene's note said that geographic documents were removed, too."

Xavier "Which could correspond to their location."

"What do your notes say?" Arabella asked, opening the notebook. She gently flipped through the pages, the entries dated five years earlier. Xavier's handwriting was impeccable, the letters formed so perfectly the notes were almost difficult to read.

"This notebook holds everything I copied from the werewolf stories," he said. He picked it up and peered at. "I wrote the last entry two days before I boarded the flight with the expedition members. I had a big pile of books and papers with me and I remember that I forgot this one by the time the dirigible was halfway over the Atlantic Ocean. Everything else I wrote is still in Antarctica."

"It was lucky then, that you forgot this."

"And that Mrs. Greene saved it," he added. "This holds much of the excised materials."

"But the materials weren't removed until last year. Why would she keep it?"

"I was acquainted with her and husband," he explained. "The mister, as she calls him outside their home. She has a passion for, well, everything. She likes knowing things. She enjoys picking other peoples' brains and learning what they know. That's why she's a librarian." He looked at the notebook a little sadly. "We're also friends and she thought I was dead. Her sentimentality may have saved us a great deal of work and frustration."

Arabella picked it up and leafed through the pages again. "What about the removal of the geographic documents? How are they related to the werewolves?"

"They contained the identifying details," Xavier said flatly, as if realizing it for the first time. "The Crown agents removed everything that would lead to someone finding out where they could be."

"Which possible locations have you written down?"

"I had dozens, but I was quite certain they would be in Scotland if they existed but we could look at the documents still available and cross-reference them with my notes. Whichever is missing should provide some clues," Xavier said.

He looked excited, and Arabella couldn't help but share the feeling. When was the last time she had seen him in his academic element? Never. "Just tell me what I'm supposed to look for," she said.

They left their room and returned to the endless sea of bookshelves. Xavier led her to another room, this one partially lit by a street-level, lace-curtained window, that held shelves of scrolls and documents protected by leather covers.

The light here was better, too, and the room didn't have the suffocating feeling Arabella experienced with the books. Unfortunately, almost everything looked the same to her.

"Do you read any languages other than English?" Xavier asked.

"I speak enough French, Spanish, and Italian to get by at airfields and restaurants but I don't read them terribly well."

That earned a smile from him. "I'll ask you to look at the English language land documents over there," he said, pointing to the far wall under the window. "I was focusing on the years 1500 to 1700. Everything is arranged by year."

"Are these really from the 1500s?" she asked dubiously.

"They're copies," he explained. "The originals are in secured areas that a mere professor would never have access to. I'm looking for land claims and legal agreements between the landowner and Westminster with unusual stipulations."

"Or missing files."

"Yes, look for missing years to start."

Arabella looked at the shelves in front of her, at the embossed leather covers. There were hundreds, if not thousands. She fought back a sigh. She could do this. She climbed the ladder in the middle of the shelves to peer at the topmost one to find a folder labeled "1460." She grabbed the edge of the shelf and urged the ladder to the right on its rails until she reached the 1500s.

"You could climb down and move the ladder that way," Xavier said from behind her.

"And spoil the fun? Never. I slide down banisters when I can get away with it, too." She picked up a folder labeled "1500." "I'm careful about the documents, I promise."

Arabella wasn't sure how much time passed, although the sunlight grew brighter through the curtained window as the morning turned into afternoon. She had found property-related files for consecutive years until the mid-

1600s, with nothing that looked amiss according to Xavier. She couldn't be entirely sure; even though he said she was with the English-language files, much of what she tried to read was barely understandable to her modern tastes. She tossed aside the completed file for 1653. "Do you speak any other languages?"

"Not completely fluently, but I have a working knowledge of a few." He set aside a folder, sending a dust cloud into his face. He sneezed. "I'm fairly proficient in Latin and can carry a conversation about the weather in Welsh."

"Why Welsh?"

"Wales is where a lot of dragon legends originate. I had at least one Welsh grandparent, but all of them died before I was born."

Arabella immediately felt like an idiot. Of course, that was where dragons would be, if they existed. "Oh."

"I can pick out a few words in Scots thanks to a couple of friends in my undergraduate years, but my accent is an insult to native speakers," he continued. "My Irish knowledge is non-existent." He picked up a couple of folders and looked back and forth between them, then set them aside. He picked up a few more. "I think I found the discrepancy."

"Really?" Arabella crossed the room to where Xavier held a bunch of faded and cracked leather folders.

"One is missing for the latter half of 1602," he said. "From Scotland."

Arabella's heart thudded. "Isn't that where you suspected the wolves might be?"

"Yes. This file's contents list an agreement regarding a travel restriction made between a barony in Scotland and Westminster. The agreement is gone, and I found the contents list in the middle of the document," he explained.

"Someone must have forgotten it when they excised the files."

"Who's it for?"

"A barony called Roseheath, led by one MacAmhlaidh, now MacAulay," he said. "I've never heard of a barony's residents being restricted from leaving their lands."

"But you said the agreement was missing." Something else struck her. "Who the hell would sign a legal agreement that kept them from leaving?"

"Someone who was threatened into it," Xavier said. "Perhaps because of what they were and their shifting abilities." His voice shook. "I think I've found them." He folded the contents sheet in half and stuck it in his notebook.

Arabella gawked at him. "Are you sure?"

He nodded. "It makes the most sense. The next step is to track down a copy of Debrett's and learn more about this MacAulay barony. I've never heard of it before."

"I wonder if it's related to the flameless candles," Arabella mused.

"How so?"

"The newest ones that are *everywhere* now. They don't flicker and they last forever. They came out of nowhere about a year ago." She'd filled her dirigible with them when they were introduced to the market. Everyone she knew had, too. They were ubiquitous across Britain. "I can't believe I remembered that," she added.

Xavier picked up a library-provided flameless candle and examined it carefully. "It's made in Scotland," he said excitedly.

"Instead of a factory in the south." Arabella shared his enthusiasm.

"We should go there," Xavier said. Just as quickly, he corrected himself. "No, we should send a telegram first."

"And what shall we say?" Arabella asked. "Tell them you're a dragon shifter and if they're amenable to having a chat?"

"Of course not. I just think it would be unseemly if we dropped out of the sky in the middle of their barony. It feels rude."

He had a point.

"We could travel to Scotland," Xavier suggested. "We can make some discreet inquiries about this barony and see if this MacAulay fellow would be willing to talk to me about, I don't know, archaeological digs around his territory. Or we'll congratulate him on a successful product that's made so many lives a little easier, *something*."

Excitement welled in Arabella at the possibility of sharing such an adventure with him. "Let's go back to Vauxhall, and I'll file a flight plan."

CHAPTER 17

As the dirigible ascended in the air, Xavier felt the pull of shifting. It was even more incessant than usual, a dull, throbbing ache that demanded his attention and transformation. He wondered if it had to do with Arabella. She really was remarkable, he thought as she expertly launched her dirigible. She was at her most peaceful when she was behind the steering yokes of flying machines and in sleep. He would treasure that memory of her next to him in bed forever. But when he thought about her sleeping, he thought about her bare skin and the bite mark he'd left on her that still hadn't faded.

He stood next to her in the flight box as the vessel took off, into the warm, late afternoon sunshine, bound for an airfield just outside Aberdeen. A look at a map before they took off indicated that it was the nearest city to Roseheath, and the barony itself could be accessed via carriage or steam cab. According to the Vauxhall airfield's comptroller, a telegraph line was recently installed within the barony limits, and they planned to send a wire from the airfield after they arrived. It felt like things were finally working out in his favor. *Their* favor, he quickly corrected himself. He wasn't alone in this anymore. He couldn't keep a smile off his face as he thought about that.

Catching his expression, Arabella asked, "What is it?"

"Can't a man be happy?" He wrapped his arm around her, hand nestled in the small of her waist.

"Even though we don't have many more answers about your condition yet?"

He shrugged. "I want them, but I don't feel as, I don't know, consumed with curiosity about it." He chose his next words carefully, not wanting to scare her off with the intensity of his feelings. "I can't tell you the relief I feel sharing this with someone. I didn't realize what a proverbial millstone was around my neck until I told you."

She gave him a look that clearly questioned his intelligence. "I beg your pardon? You faked your death and ran away to Antarctica!"

"Let me add to that. I didn't realize how freeing it would feel to share that part of me with someone." Was that unburdening on her too much? He hoped not.

"I understand that." The dirigible trembled a little as the dirigible rose a little further into the air. "I'm so used to being alone these days that having a companion is a novelty. My father and I used to travel together from the time my mother passed away. Since he remarried I've been on my own. I didn't have a chance to form friendships with other children when I was young, and you can see how my social skills have turned out since then."

"You mean your directness? I like that."

She smiled at him, a sight that he didn't think would ever not make his heart do a little flip-flop. "Not a lot of people do."

"I like everything about you."

"If you keep telling me nice things like that, you'll never be free of me, and then where will you hide away?"

Even though his dragon was the whole reason for the position they were in, it already mourned the possibility of being away from her. Was she expecting an answer? Probably. "I don't know," he said.

Inside him, his dragon bristled and roared to be let out. *Liar,* it snarled. *You can never leave her.*

XAVIER HAD BEEN TWITCHIER than usual during the flight, which Arabella was coming to recognize as a sign that he needed to shift. He paced the short length of the flight box until Arabella thought she might go insane from the sound of his bootheels against the scuffed wood floors.

"I'm sure there will be a safe place for you to shift somewhere in Aberdeen," she said. "We'll be there in about an hour and a half, and it will be dark by then. There can't be people along the entire coastline. No one spotted you in Torquay."

"It's bizarre," Xavier said. "I haven't felt like this ever."

"Maybe it's because you have to be more controlled now that you can't shift whenever you want to."

He shook his head. "I don't think it's that." His gaze darkened in the light offered by the flight box's hurricane lamps. "I think it has to do with you."

The intensity in his expression made something flip flop inside her. She tried to keep her voice even. "How so?"

"I don't know. I feel like shifting and, I don't know, breathing fire just because I can, so everyone knows you're mine. It's a different urge than usual. I think it might have to do with last night." He colored.

Her heart turned over again at the mention of being his. "I'd really like to repeat last night, if you're willing."

He barked out a harsh laugh. "Oh, God, you have no fucking idea."

"I would, actually. I was there, remember?"

His arms slid around her waist and pulled her closer to him. "I'm not usually like that."

She smoothed out a wrinkle on his coat's lapel. "Well, you can be like that with me. I *want* you to be." The whole experience had been otherworldly for her, as if she'd been claimed. She supposed she had. He'd already marked her, she remembered. Without thinking, she touched the bite mark on her neck that still hadn't faded.

Xavier's expression darkened.

"It's nothing," Arabella said before he could speak. "It's just a love bite, is all."

"It doesn't look like that to me." She heard the pain in his voice, the shame, and it pulled at heart as he looked away.

"Xavier." She gently took hold of his head in her hands. "Look at me."

He obliged.

"I'm not upset about it." She stroked the side of his face, wishing she could smooth away the worry lines bracketing his eyes as easily as she could his lapel. "Nothing happened last night that I didn't want to happen." He opened his mouth, as if to argue, but she continued. "You were very attentive to my needs, and I enjoyed every second of it. Including this." She let go of him to gesture to the mark. "Neither of us have seen this happen before. It's one of the reasons we have to find this baron."

He pressed his forehead against hers. "What if I hurt you?"

"You didn't."

"But the mark…"

"We'll find out what it is when we find the baron."

His next words were strained, his voice nearly hoarse with emotion. "What if I turned you into a dragon?"

Arabella stilled. Xavier pulled away from her, but she regained her senses and grabbed his hands. "Then I'd be the same as I am now, except I can change shape and breathe fire. As long as I stay away from the dirigible, I would be fine." She squeezed his fingers. "And you wouldn't be alone anymore, either." She couldn't believe she hadn't considered the possibility of his turning her before. Possibilities raced through her mind. "I have the dirigible," she said. "We could move from place to place and shift when we need to. It wouldn't be all bad."

"Arabella…"

"I'm telling you now that I don't want to return to Antarctica. I'll go with you for a holiday if you really want to go, but I refuse to live there." When she thought of Antarctica, she thought of his lair and how she'd forced him away from it, then of his hoarding silverware under her mattress. "When does the urge to steal anything shiny start? Or the actual shifting?"

"I don't know."

Then he was kissing her with a passion so fierce she forgot she was supposed to be keeping her attention on the skies. Her knees went weak and she thought if he wasn't holding her as tightly as he was, she might have slid to the deck. It wasn't until he backed her against the flight box's glass wall that she could catch her breath, and she realized he was crying. Alarm threaded through her. "What's wrong?"

He wrapped her in a hug, pressing his face into her hair. "Nothing that we haven't already talked about. You're truly not going to push me overboard for possibly infecting you?"

"Of course not. In retrospect, we probably should have discussed that, but we were both distracted last night." The look on his face tore at her. For the first time, she saw the self-loathing reflected in his eyes, his shame and loneliness and for what? A condition he couldn't help and overcompensated for to keep everyone else safe? "Look, if I turn out to be a dragon, then at least I'll have someone to guide me through the experience," she said. "I told you that you're not alone in this anymore, and I mean it. We're friends. Friends don't give up on each other."

"I don't usually do with my friends what I've done to you."

"Only sometimes?" She didn't try to hide the teasing note in her voice.

"Never, actually. My feelings could be hardly classified as merely friendly."

That rough undercurrent in his voice had returned, the same one he'd had the night before in the garden. Electric current of awareness and desire coursed through her, and for a moment she wished she could land her dirigible immediately and forget about their responsibilities for a while. The impulse grew stronger when he lightly nipped at her earlobe. A moan escaped her just as the dirigible tilted portside. "Damn!" She reluctantly pulled away from him to put her hands back on the yoke. Checking the equipment, she saw nothing was amiss but still kept her gaze trained on the skies ahead. "You have an unnerving ability to distract me. Use it wisely."

Xavier stood behind her and wrapped his arms around her waist.

Arabella leaned back into him, needing his stability

and warmth at her back as much as she needed to not be distracted. "Have you been to Aberdeen before?"

"A couple of times. I studied eurypterids found in the area a few years ago."

"Do I want to know what that is? Their name makes them sound like they go bump in the night."

"A prehistoric scorpion."

She shuddered. "Ugh."

His hand trailed down her hip and pulled her closer against him, drawing a gasp from her. He pressed himself against her back, and she had the distinct impression he wasn't thinking about prehistoric scorpions in that moment. "I should probably leave you to it," he said into her hair.

"If you can behave yourself, you're welcome to stay right there. We aren't going so high that I need to let the dirigible run on helium for the journey." For a distance this relatively short, she would be keeping the dirigible closer to the ground, not among the clouds where it could get by on wind power. She would have to rely on her navigation skills and sight to keep the vessel in the air.

"I always behave myself."

"Liar. I'd like you to recall the garden last night. The garden that belongs to a viscount, I should add."

"All right, I behave myself when the situation calls for it, such as my lover piloting a dirigible in low skies." His breath ruffled her hair, and she wished she didn't have to focus on the flight ahead. "I wish we could have a few days to ourselves."

Her breath caught again. "Oh?"

"Just away from everyone and without any worries about shifting or dragons. Like a normal couple."

Something inside her warmed when he spoke of their being together, his hints at wanting something more with her. Maybe staying with her. She did, too, which was unusual. Arabella had never been inclined toward settling down with someone longer than a short spell, nor had she ever cared for picking a place and setting down roots. She still wasn't crazy about the idea of settling down but traveling with someone—with Xavier—held a great deal of appeal. She hadn't ever fallen for anyone, wasn't sure she was capable of it, but she found herself in that situation with him. What was more, he appeared to reciprocate. It was a heady feeling, almost scary. "We could stay in Aberdeen for a couple of days after we find the werewolves," she said. "We could rent a room in an inn if you'd like a change of scenery from the dirigible. How much time did you plan on spending out of bed?"

He gave a strangled laugh behind her.

"I'm serious. You have to tell me how much time you want to spend looking at prehistoric scorpions and I'll find a way to amuse myself while you're doing that."

"Honestly, the thought of looking at eurypterids hadn't crossed my mind. I've been thinking about you and the werewolves almost exclusively."

"Almost? Not entirely?"

He hesitated for half a second before replying. "Exclusively. I've been thinking about you exclusively."

THE SUN HAD STARTED SETTING when they reached the Aberdeen airfield in the evening. Its golden orange glow made the airfield look like a scene from a painting, a peaceful sight that brought Xavier a small measure of comfort to look at. Then he remembered why he was here and his appreciation evaporated.

He'd lied to Arabella when he told her that he couldn't stop thinking about only her.

He couldn't push away the possibility that he'd infected her with his curse from his mind. Was that mark he left on her a sign? Would she transform into a dragon at some horrible, inopportune time when she wasn't prepared for it? He knew full well the terror an unexpected shift could cause. Yet, a selfish part of him perked up at the idea of no longer being the only dragon in existence. Of no longer being alone. The rational, moral part of him couldn't stop fretting over the possibility of sentencing someone he was in love with to his fate. He sneaked a glance at her as she focused on landing and anchoring the dirigible.

Her face was a mask of concentration, but her gaze flicked to his and gave him a quick smile that tugged at his heart.

He didn't think he'd ever been in love with someone before, and he wasn't sure he liked the feeling. He worried about her and what he might have done to her too much to enjoy it.

Once the dirigible was secured to its assigned dock, Arabella sighed and stretched. "Let's send a telegram," she suggested. "Then we'll find somewhere for supper and scout out a place for you to shift tonight."

"There's too much town here to do that safely." His dragon protested inside him as he said the words, even though it knew they were true.

Arabella shrugged. "There are loads of beaches along the coast. There's bound to be somewhere in the middle of the night that you can shift safely. I'll be your lookout, same as last time."

She said the words so casually, but they felt like a balm to his soul, one he wasn't entitled to. "Thank you," he managed.

She responded with a kiss, a gesture he already knew he would never tire of, before taking his hand and leading him away from the dirigible to the airfield office.

Once the dirigible was registered and checked in, they lingered over the telegram forms, unsure how to phrase their message to the MacAulays of the Roseheath barony. "What about, 'we request your permission to dig up your property for fossils'?" Arabella whispered. Her hand gripped the provided pencil, lingering over the paper.

"That sounds like we'll make a mess."

"What about, 'we request your permission to take samples from the barony' instead? Or something about visiting and taking some weeds for study?"

Now it was Xavier's turn to shrug. "It's as good an excuse as any. I can't think of any other reason why a pair of Londoners would come knocking at their door if not for scientific reasons."

Satisfied with his answer, Arabella wrote a short message on the slip and returned it to the comptroller. "And now, we have to wait," she said as they walked out of the office. "I hate waiting."

"I think I hate it now, too. I used to be a very patient man." He thought about his impending need to shift and how irritated his dragon was that he had to put it off. "Or perhaps it wasn't tested as often as it is now." He tightened his hold on her arm that rested in his. "I'm hungry and looking forward to supper."

"And other evening activities."

He didn't miss the suggestive note in her voice. "And other evening activities," he repeated. "Do you fancy accompanying me to the beach tonight?"

CHAPTER 18

*A*s was the case when Xavier needed to shift in Torquay, Arabella remained on the beach and watched him in dragon form under the moonlight. He stayed close to the water so he could easily dive in and hide should any humans stroll along the beach. But at half-past three in the morning, there weren't any onlookers nearby.

They had napped for a couple of hours after supper, and Arabella found now herself wide awake from her spot in the sand. All she could hear was the peaceful lap of the water against the sandbar and the occasional splash as Xavier dove into it.

It looked fun. She wondered when or if she would start to change, too.

She had been an idiot and brought it up over supper. Xavier closed off again at the idea. It didn't seem so terrible an ability to have, not when one had a companion and a place to shift. The water was too brisk to consider a swim, although she doubted Xavier would have approved of late night swimming, anyway. So, she stayed on the sand and watched him until he returned to the beach, shaking

177

water off his wings. He transformed back into his human form, his naked body in the moonlight reminding Arabella of a sculpture. Albeit a sculpture who was very much alive and looked at her with a promise in his eyes when she handed him a towel and his clothes. In her other hand was a flameless candle, one of the models produced in the Roseheath barony, but she didn't care about that as Xavier dressed.

"I thought about ravishing you on the beach," he said as they started the walk back to the airfield.

A shiver raced through her at the suggestion. "Why didn't you?"

"It's chilly by the seaside, for one," he replied. "For another, I'm sure lovemaking in the sand and rocks really isn't as exciting as it sounds… why are you looking at me like that?"

Arabella thought he sounded just as mad as he thought she looked. "I'd hardly call what we do 'lovemaking.' And please don't ever use that term again."

"I thought it would be more polite."

"There's nothing polite about it, and I wouldn't want it to be." She threaded her fingers through his as they walked along the beach to a dusty dirt road. "I like it when you're rough around the edges."

He stopped on the hard-packed road and set down his lantern. Without another word, he covered her mouth with his in a kiss that left her weak in the knees. "Are you sure I can't convince you to go back to the beach?" he murmured against her lips.

Arabella was sorely tempted. "I don't think we're far enough away from civilization for that to be a good idea."

"Yet here I am, shifting into a mythological creature." His fingers traced the lines of her jaw. She leaned into him, wanting more but unable to give or take it.

"Yes, and you take less time shifting than it would for us to find our clothes again."

"You're not as reckless as I thought you might be," Xavier remarked. He picked up his lantern and they set off again.

"And you're the polar opposite. I never would have pinned you as someone who would like that kind of risk in public."

"It's less risky than traveling alone to Antarctica in the middle of winter."

"I wouldn't have been naked if something went wrong in Antarctica."

He squeezed her hand. "Well, the sooner we get back to the dirigible, the sooner we can get naked again." He nipped at her ear, drawing a squeak from her.

It was a faster walk back to the airfield than to the beach. Arabella's body thrummed with anticipation. Whenever she stole a glance at Xavier, she saw the same hungry look on his face that he'd had the night before, a predator after his prey. Which he was, in a sense. She didn't mind the idea at all.

The airfield's electric lights glowed, blotting out the moon and stars. She felt like they were on display as they threaded through the rows of anchored dirigibles and ornithopters. Now and then, she caught the whiff of tobacco smoke. A few people milled about on the deck of a particularly large dirigible, the sounds of drunken laughter falling around them like the dew already in the air.

Not one of them had any idea that just a little while ago, only a little over a mile away, a dragon had flown around the beach and dunked himself in the water.

As soon as the exterior door was secured behind them and Arabella switched on a lamp, Xavier reached for her.

Just like the night before, he was confident and deliberate, a man who knew what he wanted.

They hadn't made it to her bedroom before he pulled at her clothes. He smelled of smoke and fire, a scent she was growing to love. It mingled with the sea and beneath it, the tantalizing fragrance of his skin. She didn't think she could ever tire of it.

This time, she was the aggressor, urging him against the sofa until he sat down with a thump. Surprise crossed his face, but was quickly replaced with the same hungry look he'd had before. He pulled her with him and she landed on his chest with an undignified "Oof!" and her arm caught in the sleeve of her half-unbuttoned blouse.

Amber eyes met hers through his spectacles, dark with desire in the low light offered by the hurricane lamp.

There was something else in his gaze, something warm and affectionate. For half a moment, she forgot about her need to get both of them naked as soon as possible and enjoyed just being cared for. Like she mattered. She reached for his spectacles and gently pulled them off his face. "Can you still see me?" she asked as she set them aside on a nearby chair. She straightened a little, straddling his hips.

"Of course." He ran a hand through her hair, now disheveled and mostly fallen out of its braid. "I'll always be able to see you." He pulled on her hair, not hard enough to hurt but just enough to urge her face closer to his.

His kiss was hot and insistent, his hands pushing her blouse off her shoulders. Arabella pulled away and worked the buttons of his shirt, hastily fastened after his shift, and then his trousers. The memory of the night before, combined with the near certainty of a repeat performance, had her coiled tight as a spring, ready to unfurl and pop out at any second.

He'd been so generous before. She wanted to return his affections.

With shaking fingers, she unbuttoned the placket on his trousers. She pushed the sides of his shirt apart, then kissed a slow trail down his chest, drawing a shudder from him. His hands fisted in her hair and he moaned, a sound that reverberated through her. She pushed his clothes further down his hips and raised her head to give him a knowing smile.

He trembled beneath her, his breath ragged as he impatiently shoved the rest of his clothes out of the way.

Save for his shirt, he was naked and just as beautiful as she remembered. A thrill coursed through her at what was still yet to happen. She lowered her head again, tongue trailing along his skin until she reached the part of him that begged for attention. Experimentally, she dragged her tongue along it before taking him in her mouth.

Xavier groaned again and grabbed her hair, his name on her lips.

She wrapped her hand around the base of his cock, moving in time to a rhythm he set as his hips undulated against her. It wasn't long before he urged her up his body and tugged at her clothes. "I don't want to finish like this," he said, his voice a scratchy rasp. "Not like this."

Arabella helped him, not wanting to tear her flight clothes. As if he could read her mind, his eye caught hers and he murmured, "I only ruin evening clothes. I like how you look in trousers too much to destroy them."

"I thought you liked the dress?" She stood up long enough to shove her trousers down her legs and kick them away before straddling him again. His skin was hot beneath hers, a tease that nearly drove her mad.

"I do. I like you in everything." He pulled her head down for a kiss, tongue demanding entrance that she was

181

only too happy to give. "But I like it best when you look like yourself. Like the woman who crashed into my mountain."

Arabella angled herself over him, stroking his cock between them before she lowered her body on to his, the feel of him inside her a welcome invasion and relief. Xavier's head rolled back, and he gripped her hips as he thrust into her. Slowly at first, building up a momentum that Arabella could tell would push her over the edge faster than she expected.

Xavier looked like he was close, too, and his breaths were closer together. She leaned down and kissed him as her orgasm crashed into her, catching his lower lip between her teeth. That motion did him in and he tightened his hold on her, thrusting greedily into her until he was spent.

For a few seconds, neither of them moved. Arabella lay against him as their hearts beat in tandem. She pressed a kiss against the hollow of his throat, too boneless to move. She wasn't sure how much time passed before Xavier shifted and moved her aside, then stood. Without another word, he scooped her up in his arms and carried her to the bedroom, setting her down in the unmade bed before climbing in next to her. She snuggled against him, sure that there was no better place in the world to be at that moment.

CHAPTER 19

Xavier and Arabella overslept the next morning, a welcome indulgence. He still couldn't deny the luxury of waking up to late morning sunlight streaming through the bedroom porthole, casting a warm glow over the woman curled up in bed beside him. A glance at the clock mounted to the wall told him it was half-past eleven. Taking care not to disturb Arabella, Xavier stealthily climbed out of bed. Breakfast was their most immediate need, he decided. That, and to see if there was a telegram waiting for them from the barony at the airfield office.

He washed and dressed, then left a note in the kitchen for Arabella in case she woke up before he returned. Then he headed out into the summer sunshine for the airfield office. There was an on-site bakery, he recalled from the night before. He doubted Arabella would reject croissants served in bed.

A telegram waited for them at the office, just as he hoped. The clerk pushed the paper across the counter, a bored expression on his face, before turning back to his newspaper. With shaking hands, Xavier accepted it and briefly pondered if he should wait to open the envelope before he returned to the dirigible.

I could have a coronary and drop dead before I ever got to read it. Or I could lose it.

That decided it for him. He unsealed the envelope and removed the telegram.

ROSEHEATH WELCOMES FOSSIL HUNTERS STOP DIRIGIBLES CANNOT BE ACCOMMO-DATED STOP

It took Xavier a few seconds to remember the pretense he and Arabella had come up with to gain access to the barony. He was supposed to be interested in digging things up, after all but no dirigibles? How were they to reach the barony otherwise? He didn't know how to drive a steam vehicle, not that he knew the Scottish countryside, anyway. He was also unsure if he and Arabella would be able to rent a carriage and team of horses, and there was still the treacherous landscape ahead of them to consider with that option, too. He folded up the telegram and stuck it in his trouser pocket. He'd have to ask Arabella what she thought.

He returned to the dirigible with chocolate croissants in hand, just in time to see her puttering about the galley wearing only his shirt. It was a frustratingly distracting sight and he nearly dropped the package of croissants.

"Tea?" she asked by way of greeting.

"Of course." Before he could pour himself a cup, she kissed him, and once again he forgot everything else. It wasn't until she pulled away and poured him a cup from her battered tin teapot that he remembered the telegram. "I come bearing breakfast and this," he announced, and held out the telegram to her.

Arabella quickly scanned it. "Well, that's a pain in the arse, if we can't take the dirigible."

"Do you know how to drive?"

"I don't, but the telegram only says no dirigibles. It doesn't say anything about an ornithopter. They're available to rent in town." She sipped her tea. "Unless you want to fly there with me on your back."

"I'd like to try that sometime, but I don't think today is the day."

"Ugh, you're a spoilsport." She sniffed. "Do I smell pastries?"

"You do. With chocolate, even." He set the package on the small sideboard and opened it. The smell of butter and chocolate rose in the air.

"Mmm, thank you." She picked up the entire package and headed back to the bedroom. "Come back to bed with me."

Xavier didn't need to be told twice. He shoved the telegram back into his pocket, and followed her to the bedroom.

BY THE EARLY AFTERNOON, Arabella and Xavier were airborne in a bulky rented ornithopter.

Not an hour into their flight, she was already regretting it and silently cursing Roseheath for not allowing them to arrive by dirigible. The vessel's wings creaked and made the passenger basket bounce in a way that had her stomach protesting. A glance at Xavier told her he felt as much the same. The steam-powered engine was much too loud, making conversation impossible but she was still able to fly the blasted thing with minimal difficulty. She had to admit the views beneath them were lovely, just as they were on the beach the night before. It was refreshing to see a landscape that wasn't crowded with telegraph poles and roofs, their chimney belching black smoke. Even the air smelled cleaner. Despite the noise, she couldn't help but shout to Xavier, "I still wish you could've flown us there."

"And offend or terrify our werewolf hosts?" he yelled back. He adjusted his flight goggles. "Not to mention the human locals?"

"I'm certain that if you fly fast enough and high enough, someone might mistake you for a particularly unusual ornithopter instead." A small insect flew into her mouth at her last word, making her gag. The ornithopter lurched to the side. Xavier reached over for the steering yoke and righted the vessel.

"That's happened to me twice already," he yelled.

Ugh. She nodded, irritated that even a shouted conversation was off the menu if it meant swallowing bugs. Why the hell were they this far up in the air, anyway? She shuddered.

Xavier smiled and gave her shoulder a reassuring squeeze.

Keeping her lips firmly clamped together, she trained her gaze on the landscape ahead. The ornithopter cut through the air like a dull knife trying to cut through a potato, choppy and awkward, never gaining the grace her dirigible did when it hit the skies. Its passenger basket was too small to have any seating, so she and Xavier remained on their feet as it bounced and lurched. The slightest gusts of wind bounced and dropped them a few heart-stopping feet. Arabella silently cursed Roseheath for their refusal to allow dirigibles to drop anchor anywhere in the barony. She landed the ornithopter at the foot of a hill, its drive leading to an old-fashioned grand manor straight out of a gothic novel. Thick shrubbery and brambles lined either side of the drive, thistles in bloom at the edges. When she and Xavier left the passenger basket, swaying on their feet as they regained their sense of balance, she noticed that the whole area looked like something out of such a book that she would never read.

A new-looking wooden sign at the foot of the drive announced the property as Roseheath Manor, the seat of the barony. "I suppose we've arrived," Xavier said, peeling off his flight goggles. They left red marks around his eyes, and Arabella was sure she had the same when she took off hers. He slipped on his spectacles and blinked as his vision adjusted.

"I hope they're friendly," she replied.

Xavier reached into the basket for his satchel, something he purchased in a secondhand shop before they left London. Inside was a notebook, pencils, and a few cheap brushes to keep up the pretense of looking for fossils. He swung its leather strap over his shoulder, then reached for Arabella's hand.

A swarm of butterflies unleashed themselves in her stomach. "I think I'm more nervous now than when I was flying to Antarctica," she announced as they started the walk up the drive.

"It isn't unreasonable to have a healthy amount of fear. We could very well be walking into a den of wolves. That would give anyone pause for discomfort."

What if the werewolves weren't as friendly as Xavier was, if the pack actually existed? What if they sniffed out their ruse before they could bring up the subject of shifters? It would be easy enough to hide a couple of bodies in this part of the country. Did wolves eat people? Arabella racked her brain, trying to remember the scant information she knew about the animals. Xavier would probably know. "What do wolves eat?"

"They're carnivores, so meat."

"Does that include humans?"

He stopped in his tracks. So did Arabella. "I don't believe so," he said slowly. He looked up the drive, at the house that stood atop it. "But I'm not certain."

Frustration welled up inside her. Not for the first time, she hadn't done enough research before taking off for a new adventure. Like her trip to Antarctica nearly was, this could prove to be a fatal journey. "Damn it!" she snapped. She had to force herself not to stamp her foot in fury like a child.

"What is it?" Xavier's concern was palpable. "Did you see something?"

"No. I'm angry that once again, I haven't prepared. We know nothing about wolves and we're walking into their territory. No one knew we were coming here, so if something happens, no one will look for us." The bushes trembled to their left. An undignified yelp escaped her before a rabbit dashed across the drive.

"We've left a trail," Xavier explained patiently. "There are flight records and the Aberdeen shop has your name for the ornithopter rental."

"Ornithopters crash and disappear. So do people."

"Arabella, I won't let anything happen to you," he said firmly. "That's a promise. I have the means of keeping you safe, and I will utilize them if necessary." He leaned his forehead against hers, his voice a rasp. "I would kill for you if I had to."

His confession made her breath catch. "You would?"

"I'd risk people seeing me like that, if it meant I could keep you safe."

She shouldn't be as thrilled or relieved as she was to hear his violent declaration, but she was. Impulsively, she kissed him.

His response was immediate, his body stiffening against hers as he gripped her hips, pulling her closer to him. The crazy thought of hiding in the bushes to fuck popped in her mind, only to be quickly tempered when she remembered the brambles and thistles. It also seemed impolite to do such a thing when they were on this mission, even by her relaxed moral standards.

"I love you, Arabella," he said against her lips.

The words—unexpected, but so dearly wanted—had her pulling away from him just enough to scan his face. She could hardly believe him. "You do?"

"I have no right to, but yes."

"No." She put a finger over his lips. "Do *not* start getting melodramatic with me. You have every right to." He tried to open his mouth to protest, but she didn't move her finger.

He gently bit it instead, sending a shudder of pleasure through her.

"I love you, too," she said softly.

His eyes went wide before he tightened his hold on her, lips sealing against hers.

She breathed him in, not wanting the moment to end, a moan escaping her when his tongue demanded entrance to her mouth. Dimly, she was aware of the sound of brambles brushing against each other next to the drive and remembered the rabbit.

Something rushed from the bushes and knocked Xavier to his feet, so fast it was a blur. It took a couple of seconds for the sight of something huge and covered in shaggy fur to register.

Her scream was loud enough to distract the creature, who turned a snarling face to her. "Oh, my God," she breathed. It was an honest to God werewolf. Regular wolves couldn't possibly be this huge, nor did she think they had the human intelligence in their eyes that this one did.

Its jaws snapped at her, and it was distracted for just long enough for Xavier to regain his footing. He ripped off his clothes with an inhuman speed, and Arabella had the distinct impression that he was about to do what he promised earlier.

At the sound of Xavier's clothes hitting the ground, the werewolf whipped its head in his direction and lunged.

Xavier's shift was quick and brutal, the fastest Arabella had ever seen. He filled the drive in a matter of seconds, scales shining in the early summer sun, nostrils flaring smoke. His wings touched the brambles on either side of the drive. With a casual flick of his clawed foot, he tossed the werewolf into the brambles as if the beast was lighter than a fly.

Pride surged in her at the sight.

The werewolf squealed in pain and surprise, but quickly found his feet. Moving fast for an injured animal, he sank his teeth into Xavier's foot.

Xavier roared, the sound louder than any scream Arabella could produce, and belched a small cloud of fire. She fell to the ground to avoid it, landing on a patch of thistles. "Fuck!" she yelled. "Both of you, stop it!"

Growls issued from both of their throats. The werewolf snarled.

"We aren't here to hurt you," Arabella said. "Xavier, please don't burn anything down. We came here looking for answers and we aren't going to reveal your secrets."

The werewolf's gaze flicked to Arabella. She slowly rose to her feet, unsure how to respond. Was she supposed to look away from the wolf, to show deference? Wasn't that how it worked with predators?

The werewolf sat back on its haunches, looking at her and Xavier as if trying to decide what to do next.

Xavier stayed where he was, belly low to the ground, ready to attack.

"Why doesn't everyone get back into their human form?" she said. Her voice was steadier than she expected, and she hoped they felt as reassured as she sounded. "I think we have a lot to talk about."

The werewolf inclined his head toward the manor.

"Should we follow?" Arabella asked.

The beast nodded.

"Are you going to kill us?"

It tilted its head to the side.

"Is that a maybe?"

That didn't earn a response, although she could've sworn it rolled its eyes.

"We aren't here to hurt you," she repeated. "I promise. Although I'm sure you've already guessed that we aren't here to survey the barony for fossils."

With a groan, Xavier shifted back into his human form. He picked up his discarded clothes and the werewolf turned away to give him privacy. "Appreciated," Xavier said. He looked down at the bite on his leg, already healing.

The werewolf trotted a few feet ahead of them. "We'll be right there," Arabella called.

Xavier quickly dressed, wincing as his trousers touched the bite and scratches from the werewolf's claws. Arabella came close to muttering something about making a new rug for the dirigible but held her tongue. Who knew how many other werewolves were hiding in the brambles? "Are you all right?" she whispered as they resumed their walk.

"I will be in a few minutes when everything's healed," he replied. He squeezed her hand and gave her a quick smile. She supposed he'd earned it. He'd just won a fight with a werewolf, after all.

The werewolf waited for them, then walked a couple of feet ahead until they reached the top of the drive. Up close, the manor was magnificent: an older, stately home that was in the throes of restoration. New stonework had recently been installed on its exterior, contrasting with the weather beaten original part of the home, and the roof looked new.

The front door opened, and a young woman ran down the steps in a swirl of light blue skirts. "Henry!" she screamed.

Terror was written across her face, a fear so intense that it broke Arabella's heart.

"What's going on?" she demanded. Her gaze searched Arabella and Xavier's faces. "Who are you?"

Her accent was English, from a good part of London, which surprised Arabella. "We came here looking for werewolves," she said.

The Englishwoman let out a sob. The werewolf nuzzled her skirted legs with his face, and she reached for his shaggy fur, burying her fingers into it.

"It's not like that," Xavier quickly said. Indecision warred on his face, and Arabella briefly wondered what he was thinking about. "My name is Dr. Xavier Kinnon," he continued. "I came here looking for answers about what I am."

The woman peered at him, then haltingly asked, "Are you a werewolf, too?"

"No, madam," he replied. "I'm a dragon."

CHAPTER 20

Xavier and Arabella were seated in a parlor on a worn green velvet sofa, the fabric bald in spots. It was another contrast in this house full of the new and falling apart. The ceiling was new-looking, but the yellowed wallpaper was peeling in places. It was an odd contradiction for nobility.

Seated across from them was the woman, who introduced herself as Lady Adelle MacAulay, Baroness Roseheath once Xavier's identity as a shifter was established. Lady Adelle kept her hands clasped in her lap and an uncertain smile on her face as their housekeeper fussed around them, offering tea with biscuits. They were still waiting for the werewolf himself, the baron to appear in his human form.

He did a few minutes later, dark blond hair wild around his head and a feral look on his face. His shirt wasn't buttoned correctly, but no one commented on it.

Xavier immediately stood up and held out his hand. Just as quickly, he felt like an idiot. He wasn't sure how to address a baron he hadn't already been introduced to.

The werewolf didn't seem to care when he shook it heartily. "Henry MacAulay," he said, not bothering with his title.

"Xavier Kinnon."

"I see you've met my wife, Adelle." The baron gave her a soft look that belied his wild appearance before sitting in a chair next to her.

Xavier nodded. "This is my companion, Miss Arabella Greaves."

The housekeeper bustled into the room again, this time bearing a tray of sandwiches. "I'm sure you're hungrier than usual," she muttered under her breath to the baron. To the baroness, she said, "And you, too." She turned a sharp eye to Xavier. "I'm sure you are, as well. Shifting takes a lot out of a man."

"It does, indeed." Now that Xavier wasn't so worried that he and Arabella would be mauled to death by were-wolves, he realized he was starving. Their long-ago late breakfast of croissants and sex was forgotten, and he looked at the tray longingly.

The housekeeper left them, and the baron and baroness helped themselves.

Xavier and Arabella followed suit after a moment.

"Nothing's been poisoned," Henry said when he saw them hesitate.

"That thought hadn't occurred to me."

"We're fine to serve ourselves here," Adelle remarked. To Xavier and Arabella, she said, "If you're worried about crumbs, don't be. The furniture is due to be replaced shortly."

"The whole place looks to be under renovations." It was an inane reply, but Xavier was unsure how to steer the conversation back to the existence of shifters.

Henry was the one who brought it up. "So, what is a dragon doing in our barony?"

Xavier's curiosity got the better of him. "Do you know of any others?"

To his disappointment, Henry shook his head. "I don't, sadly. I had no idea dragons were real until a quarter of an hour ago. You scared the hell out of me."

"I couldn't tell."

"I'm a werewolf who's waiting for the full moon to finally come and go. My patience is thin and my wolf is more protective than usual." He cast a meaningful glance at Adelle, who smiled back at him.

Xavier didn't understand.

Arabella nodded her head.

He was distracted by the mention of the full moon. "Is it like the stories then? You're compelled to shift?"

"I can shift whenever I want, but I have to when the moon is full. The entire barony does." He leaned back in his chair. "If you had shown up at the manor later tonight, you could have been torn apart."

"How many are here?" Arabella asked.

"Most of the village. Those that can't shift are still in on the secret." His expression darkened. "Our existence *must* stay a secret. How did you two discover us?"

Arabella squeezed his knee. Xavier sighed and took a fortifying sip of tea.

"Perhaps whiskey might be better right now," Henry said. Without another word, he stood up and crossed the room to open a carved wooden cabinet, its doors inlaid with brass. He removed an unmarked bottle half-filled with dark amber liquid and a pair of glasses. He inclined his head to Arabella. "Would you like some?"

"No, thank you. Tea is fine."

From the corner of his eye, Xavier saw Adelle shudder.

Henry set the glasses on the table between them and poured two drinks, handing one to Xavier. He sniffed at it experimentally. *What the hell are they brewing here in their stills?* Not wanting to insult his host, he took a healthy gulp and coughed, his eyes burning. It took a few seconds for him to regain his breath and voice. "Are you certain you're not trying to poison me?"

Adelle hid a smile behind her hand, although Xavier noticed she looked a little green at the scent of the liquor.

"No," replied Henry. He finished his drink as easily as if it was water.

Xavier looked at the half-inch of liquor still in his glass and tried not to retch. Holding his breath, he knocked it back and waited for the nausea to disappear. "Excellent," he lied. "Do you brew it yourself?"

"The manor's butler does. The recipe's been in Bensfort's family for generations." Henry's friendly demeanor evaporated, and his flinty expression returned. "You still haven't told me how you came to know of us."

Xavier had to start from the beginning. How he discovered he was a dragon shifter. That he had never met anyone else like him. That his academic career in paleontology was derailed when he started his research into mythology, hoping for a human connection. How he came across the old stories of a werewolf pack in Scotland. Of his opportunity to escape and fake his death in Antarctica.

Henry interrupted him when he reached the part of the story of his research into werewolves. "When was this, exactly?"

"Just over five years ago."

The baron visibly relaxed. "That material was supposed to have been removed from all archives and libraries over a year ago, when Adelle married me. It was part of a deal we made with Westminster. As part of our agreement, we don't leave Scotland. As long as they leave us be, we leave them alone." He smiled. "There are a few other stipulations, of course, but they work on our favor these days."

"The flameless candles," Arabella said.

He nodded. "They've been my most commercially successful invention. The barony and the house are finally having some long-needed repairs, as you can see." He gestured to the ceiling. "The roof finally gave up the spring before last and we had a hell of a flood in the attic. In fact..."

"Henry," murmured Adelle.

"Of course. My apologies for going off the subject." He cleared his throat. "There was an unfortunate incident with someone who found the same information you did and stormed my home demanding... well, quite a bit." He sent a possessive look Adelle's way. "His primary demand was that I turn him, which is impossible."

Xavier's heart thundered at this piece of information. "Are you saying I can't make other dragons?"

"I don't know about dragons in particular, but were-wolves can't be made, only born. We can't bite someone and make them like us."

For a moment, Xavier felt as if a half-ton weight had been lifted from his shoulders. It stood to reason that if a werewolf shifter couldn't create a new wolf with a bite, neither could a dragon. "Oh, thank God," he muttered. When he looked at Arabella, he saw she looked a little sad at the news. He made a mental note to ask her about that later.

"So, you really don't know any others of your kind?" Adelle asked gently.

"None. My parents have passed on and I don't have

any siblings or cousins that I know of." Loneliness slammed into his chest like a brick in a stocking, a hated feeling. It had been so easy to forget it when he was with Arabella.

Henry regarded him thoughtfully over the rim of his glass, recently refilled. "I wish I could be of more help. Our pack has stories of dragons from medieval times, before England forced us to stay here. They're few and far between. None of them speak of shifters. The last one I know of took place shortly after the Crusades."

Xavier's happiness at finding another shifter was tempered when he realized he might truly be the only of his kind left in the world. "Oh," he said, voice small.

"I'm sorry," Henry added.

Arabella reached for his hand.

He gripped it like it was a lifeline. "I suppose it's like red hair or odd-colored eyes," he mused. "Sometimes, a body is born with them and no one knows why." The woman with red hair sitting next to him wasn't the only person with such a feature in existence. A lump formed in his throat. He didn't try to speak. There wasn't a point. He knew he was casting a pall over the room, that everyone else in the parlor felt sorry for him.

Henry tried to lighten the mood. "Why don't you come out with our pack tonight to shift?" he asked. "I noticed that you breathed a little smoke when we were in our other forms. I will unfortunately have to ask you to refrain from that near the village itself."

"You're welcome to stay the night," Adelle added. "Now that we know you're not government agents or mercenaries." She smiled. "We have a room available for you."

"Or do you need two?" Henry asked.

"One is fine," Arabella said. She quickly glanced at

Xavier. "I apologize, I should have asked. Do you want to stay?"

Xavier 's response was immediate. "Yes."

He had never had a community before outside of the academic, who were bound together by their love of fossils. He wasn't sure he had one now, but he would take any chance he could to be part of theirs, as small as it may be.

LATER THAT EVENING, Arabella and the baroness lingered over the supper table while Xavier and Henry went outside to shift.

"Henry's usually a little gentler," Adelle said once they were out of earshot. "He'll be less tense and irritable after the full moon tonight. Another biscuit?"

"Please." Arabella accepted one from the proffered plate.

There was something she wanted to bring up with the baroness now that they were alone. Since they knew that Xavier couldn't turn Arabella into a dragon, she wanted to know what the mark he left on her meant. "I have a rather delicate question to ask," she began.

"Of course."

"Xavier bit me the other night," she continued.

Adelle's brows rose, but she didn't appear too alarmed yet. "How so?"

"Not in a... violent way." At least, not in a violent way that neither of them didn't want.

The baroness seemed to understand the implication. "*Oh.*"

"He left a mark on me," Arabella admitted. "It hasn't healed. At least, the mark hasn't gone away. It doesn't hurt." Her face burned, unused to talking about physical intimacy with a virtual stranger as she was. No, not a stranger, she reminded herself. A new friend.

"A mate mark," Adelle said.

"I beg your pardon?"

Adelle cast a quick look around the dining room, as if to reassure herself that we're still alone. She unbuttoned the high collar of her blue day dress and pulled the fabric aside to reveal a scar not unlike Arabella's. It was definitely made by human, or mostly human teeth.

Arabella's hand flew to her own scar, still covered by her flight jacket. "Yes, like that. What does it mean?"

The baroness buttoned her collar again. "It's a claim among werewolves," she said. "Perhaps it's the same with dragons. Henry did it when his wolf recognized me as his true mate. It's very sacred to wolves. It bonds you for life."

If she hadn't already been sitting down, Arabella's knees would have given way. "What?"

Stricken, Adelle explained, "It's a way shifters claim their mates. Bonding is just that, connecting a couple forever. After a time, you feel the other's emotions a little. At least, Henry and I do now." It took a couple of seconds for Arabella's reaction to register. "Oh, no."

Arabella quickly recovered. "No, I'm not upset about it. Just shocked and surprised, is all." Xavier would be devastated and angrier with himself than he already was. "We didn't know," she added. She wasn't sure she wanted to go into details about how it happened with anyone, let alone the baroness she had just met, friendly as she was. Although she suspected the baroness wouldn't have minded if she did.

"Will this be a problem for you?" Adelle asked.

"No, at least not for me. Xavier's going to be very upset, I think. He has been very clear that my willingness to be with him has to be my choice."

"I see." Adelle leaned back in her chair. "Would you like a drink?"

"From your butler's still?" Arabella shuddered at the memory of its scent. "I appreciate the offer, but no thank you."

"No offense taken. I can't handle the smell or taste myself these days." She gave Arabella a knowing look across the table. "We're expecting a baby in about five months."

"I sort of already guessed that. The baron is so protective of you."

"He's always been like that, but that possessive streak has certainly increased since we found out. Henry usually has more sense than to go out outside in his wolf form, during the day, to investigate an ornithopter at the foot of the drive."

"Congratulations to you both."

"Thank you." She beamed. "I must admit it took some time for me to get used to the idea. Now that my morning nausea has subsided a little, I'm looking forward to being a mother."

"The baby will be a werewolf?"

"MacAulay babies always are. He or she won't shift for a few years, though."

"I wonder if ours would be a dragon," she mused aloud.

"Are you expecting?"

"No," Arabella quickly replied. She had never thought much about parenthood, assuming that one day she would find a man who enjoyed flight as much as she did and have a couple of children. She'd always liked the idea of raising a pair of them. They would live aboard the dirigible, as she had grown up. "Although I'm not opposed to them." It wasn't as though she and Xavier had taken any precautions, either. She wasn't usually so irresponsible. *We should have discussed this* before *everything else happened.*

"You and Xavier will have a great deal to talk about," Adelle said, voice soft. "But please know, that at least among werewolves, claiming and marking a mate is done out of love. It's very special and very rare that shifters meet and build lives with their true mates."

Xavier was likely the only one of his kind. Rare to begin with, and near-impossible odds that he would find a mate. She needed to find him and tell him they would be all right, that neither of them would ever have to be alone again. That it was nothing short of a miracle that she'd crashed into his Antarctic den. "Where is everyone?" she asked abruptly, standing up. "I have to find Xavier."

The baroness shook her head. "It's best to wait until morning."

"Are the wolves dangerous?"

"They never have been toward me, but they won't recognize you or your scent. Stay inside for now. They're likely hunting rabbits or something, anyway." A shudder rippled through her.

Arabella sighed, a sound of frustration, before plunking back into her seat. Before she met Xavier, she would have run headfirst into a den of werewolves, consequences be damned. Running headfirst into something, disregarding all advice to the contrary was the whole reason she ended up crashed in Antarctica in the first place but she'd learned to be warier of her safety since then. She had a lot to live for now, more than crossing off countries she'd visited. "Of course," she muttered. "I think I'll take that drink now."

BEING A MAN OF SCIENCE, Xavier wasn't one to visit churches. He had to admit that the little church that served the barony was charming, and its vicar, while not a shifter, welcoming. Father Paul still made himself scarce after the sun went down and the moon appeared in the sky, bright as a newly minted penny.

With the vicar gone and Arabella confined to the manor, he wondered just how dangerous his walking into a den of wolves would be. He was surrounded by the barony's shifter residents, all looking a little feral this evening. They were friendly with him, curious about his being a dragon and his ability to shift at will. Evidently, that was a rare talent to have among shifters, save for Henry. Alpha wolves could do it whenever they wanted.

With the full moon overhead, everyone streamed outside the church, naked as the day they were born.

He found a quiet spot away from the others to shift, careful not to breathe fire or smoke. He pawed along the ground, looking for a good spot to take flight, as the werewolves' bays rang through the air.

He'd never heard a wolf's howls before. He was surprised that they didn't sound ominous or frightening, or perhaps it was simply because he knew they were human the rest of the time. The howls were chatter among old friends, reunited after a long absence. In a way, he supposed they were.

A smaller wolf bounded in his direction, then yelped in surprise when he saw Xavier. The wolf shrank back out of instinct.

Xavier tried to convey through his eyes as best he could that he was harmless, then lowered himself to the ground, bowing his head in a gesture of submission. The wolf approached again, sniffed his clawed feet, then barked and wagged his tail like a dog.

A few other wolves came a little closer as well, then joined the smaller one in barking welcomes. If Xavier's facial ability allowed it, he would have smiled in response. He followed them as they turned and ran into a forest near the church, albeit slower. He lumbered behind them, unused to running, and came to a stop when he realized his body was too big to navigate between the trees. He returned to open space, and let himself take flight. He'd never been above houses before. It was quite the view, a sharp contrast to Antarctica's endless snowy landscapes or the English beaches he hastily shifted on. He soared higher, flying around the barony, until he reached the manor house the MacAulays called home.

Arabella was inside.

He missed her desperately.

He'd told her he loved her, and he did. He wondered if he hadn't made a mistake in doing so, making her feel obligated to stay with him like a foundling she'd stumbled across.

A few lights shone in the house's windows, and he looked for the one that was likeliest to come from the second floor room he and Arabella were given for the night. It had a view of the back garden, he recalled, a few doors away from the suite the baron and baroness used.

A figure with flame-colored hair passed a window with a candle on its sill, then looked through the glass. She jumped, then smiled and gestured for him to come closer.

Xavier was only too happy to oblige.

Arabella unlatched it and opened it, reaching out to pat his scaled snout. "Are you enjoying yourself?"

Xavier gave a slight nod and leaned into her hand, small as it felt when he was in this form.

"I spoke to the baroness about the bite mark," she said,

lowering her voice to a whisper. "She says it's a mate mark."

Xavier hadn't been expecting the conversation to take that turn. His contentment with how the evening turned out evaporated. This sounded serious. He put his head through the window, intending to shift back to his human form so they could discuss the mark, but his body got stuck halfway through, too wide for the narrow frame.

"Damn it," said Arabella. She sighed. "How can I help you out?"

It took a few seconds for him to free his wings and get out of the window, back into the night. He held himself in the air, waiting for her to continue. Perhaps what she said about the mark wouldn't be too concerning.

"Werewolves mark their mates," Arabella continued. "It's a sign of love. It creates an unbreakable bond between the couple. We assumed it's the same for dragons." She smiled and stroked his face again. "We're linked together forever. There will be no one else for either of us."

Bonded by a supernatural link neither of them knew existed until that evening. It took everything Xavier had not to recoil from her touch. Not because he didn't want it —he did, more than anything—but because he didn't deserve it. In the heat of passion, he'd given in to a monstrous instinct that he could have ignored and didn't. How long would her happiness last once she truly felt the impact of what he had done? That he had trapped her, however inadvertently? He had taken away her choice to do so.

He should shift immediately, tell her what a terrible thing he had done.

Just as he'd run away from England and his whole life before, he could do it again. It would be easier for both of them if he did. It would save an argument over the mate mark, over his horror, that he'd all but branded her against her will. It would be better this way. The sight of her hopeful, happy face tore at him. He dreaded what he was about to do and hated himself for it. He backed away from the window and took flight. Her confused cry made his eyes water in a way he hadn't known he was capable of before, but he didn't look back. He sailed into the night sky, away from the barony and Arabella.

CHAPTER 21

*a*rabella stared at Xavier as he flew away. She felt as if an electric current had been run through her body, holding her in place against her will. "What the hell?" she whispered. Nothing responded to her. In a matter of seconds, Xavier had taken to the skies, away from the barony.

Why would he do that?

Was he running away again?

Hurt and frustration welled in her, finally galvanizing her into action. She bolted from the room and ran for the staircase, nearly falling down in her haste. She was stopped by the manor's housekeeper at the foot, who grabbed her arm.

"What's this about?" she asked indignantly. "You could have knocked me over!"

"I—it's complicated, I think," Arabella replied. She felt like crying. "I need to get to my ornithopter."

"Phillip brought it on the property a couple of hours ago," Mrs. Tuplin replied. "It will be waiting for you at the side of the house." Her gaze searched Arabella's face. "You understand it isn't wise to go outside right now?"

"The wolves don't eat people, do they?"

"Of course not, but they don't know you. We just don't want to see you injured."

"I don't care about that. I need to get to my ornithopter, now."

At last, Mrs. Tuplin seemed to understand Arabella's urgency. "Shall I get the lady of the manor?"

Arabella didn't want to bother the pregnant baroness at this late hour; she'd retired to her rooms not an hour ago. She might have an idea of where a stupid dragon might be hiding in this part of the country. "Please."

"I'll fetch her," Mrs. Tuplin said. "You get your flying machine ready. What's this about, if you don't mind my asking?"

"My companion is a stubborn idiot."

"I see." The housekeeper nodded.

"I might have been an idiot, too. I told him something that probably should have waited until he was back in his human form."

"Are dragons more difficult than wolves?"

Did it matter? They were wasting precious seconds. Still, Arabella didn't want to appear impolite. "I couldn't tell you. Xavier's the only dragon I've ever known and the baron the only wolf." She started walking to the foyer, eager to see the conversation over. "I'll get to my ornithopter now."

Mrs. Tuplin dashed up the stairs with remarkable speed for a woman who looked old enough to be Adelle's mother.

It wasn't until Arabella let herself out of the house's grand wooden doors and prowled the side of the property that she realized she was rushing into things like an idiot again, too. Just like she had done with the Antarctic expedition, just as she had taken to the skies as a solo aviator after her father remarried. Just as she had always done: run headfirst into something without a plan. Where the hell would she go? She didn't know this part of the country. She hardly knew Scotland at all. If she took flight now, she would be doing so blindly and would end up crashed on the side of a hill or something. There wouldn't be a dragon to save her this time.

"Arabella?" A ghostly figure appeared at the side of the house. It took a few seconds for Arabella to recognize her as the baroness, wearing a thin white nightgown under a white knitted shawl that had to be too warm for the summer weather. Her long dark hair was unbound. In her hand she held a flameless candle and a sheet of foolscap. When she handed it to Arabella, she saw it was a map. "Mrs. Tuplin said Xavier's gone?" The artificial candle's flame made her look angelic, but the effect was marred by the concern in her voice.

Arabella nodded. She opened the flight basket's door and stepped inside. "He came to our window." Just thinking about it made her want to cry. "You know, it was like something out of a fairy tale, the dragon coming to visit." She almost said "the fair maiden," but she was neither of those things. "Anyway, I told him about the mate mark and I suppose he panicked. He flew away from the house, away from the barony. I think he headed north."

Adelle hurried to the ornithopter and stepped inside the flight basket. "Well, let's look for him." She held her candle aloft, looking around the basket. "Is there somewhere we can strap ourselves in?"

"Do you seriously mean to look for him with me?"

"Of course. You don't know Roseheath. I do and I've never taken a trip in an ornithopter before. It will be an adventure."

"Are you sure you should be doing that in your condition?" Arabella strapped her flight goggles to her face.

"I'm pregnant, not helpless, and if I could survive all that vomiting in the first few months, I can survive this." The baroness shuddered. "No one told me I would be that sick."

Arabella handed her Xavier's flight goggles.

"I don't know how to navigate or fly," the baroness cautioned her.

"That's all right, I do but it will be helpful for you to direct me with the map."

"That I can do." The baroness adjusted her goggles.

Arabella wound the engine's lever until it gave a faint steamy hiss, then directed the machine into the air. Its wings flapped, shaking the flight basket in a way that could make the most experienced aviator nauseated, but the baroness only squeaked and gripped the basket's edge. Then they were airborne. Arabella directed the ornithopter in the direction Xavier had flown.

"There's a forest that runs along the barony in this direction," Adelle said, voice raised to be heard over the engine's noise. "It ends in a cliff overlooking a lake. There's a network of small caves in the area. We thought that was where you two would go to look for fossils."

That was as good a place to start looking for Xavier as any. Below them, a group of werewolves gathered and followed their path. "Should I be worried?" Arabella asked.

The baroness looked down over the edge. "I don't think so." She waved and shouted, "Everything's fine!"

The largest werewolf stood up on his hind legs and gave such a growl that Arabella could hear it, thirty feet in the air. She couldn't be sure in the light offered by the full moon, but it looked like Henry in his wolf form. All the gods in all the heavens above, she hoped he understood she wasn't trying to kidnap his wife.

Henry was the only wolf to keep following them, even as they approached the forest Adelle told her about.

Arabella directed the ornithopter higher to avoid the treetops but kept it low enough to see the ground. Unfortunately, the tree cover was too thick see it clearly. She felt like stamping her feet and swearing. As it was, she yelled out, "God damn it, Xavier, why did you have to do this? Where are you?"

Adelle took that as a cue to lean over the edge and shout, "*Xavier!*"

That was a good idea, actually. Not just to find him, but to reassure an angry werewolf that his mate wasn't being spirited away.

Both of them continued to yell Xavier's name as they flew over the forest. At one point, the baroness retched over the side and threw up. "Should I return to the manor?" Arabella asked.

Looking a little green under her candle's flame, Adelle shook her head. "No." She took a few deep, fortifying breaths. "This is more important right now."

The forest gave way to a clearing that ended in a cliff with a sharp drop off. "You mentioned there's a cave system here," Arabella said. "Shall I land here or on the beach?"

"There's a path that leads to the beach. Why don't you land here, and we'll look in the forest?"

It seemed like a sensible solution. Arabella brought the ornithopter to a halt and landed it as gently as she could.

Trees rustled, and a few moments later the naked baron appeared, unbothered by his being in the altogether. Before he could speak, Adelle rushed to his side. "We're looking for Xavier," she said hurriedly. "Arabella is going to look for him along the beach."

"It's the middle of the night!" Henry said.

"And she'll stay on the beach," Adelle added, giving a knowing look to Arabella. "We'll look for Xavier in the forest. You should shift back to your wolf form, anyway. You really do need the full experience under the moon."

"My love…"

"Please, Henry. We need to find him."

"Why the hell did he run away?"

"I'll explain that to you later. Or Arabella will, when she's returned with Xavier. He couldn't have gone very far."

Arabella wasn't so sure about that, but she nodded anyway. She looked through the ornithopter's supplies and found a small kerosene lamp, its fuel reserves full. "I'll head to the beach now."

"We'll be there shortly if Henry can't pick up Xavier's scent in the forest." The baroness gave Arabella directions to the beach, cautioning her to be careful along the path.

At least the path was brightly lit between the moon and her lantern. Arabella was still careful with her steps, boot soles a little slippery against the path's stones and sand. The beach itself was rocky and inhospitable, a sharp contrast to the one Xavier shifted on in Aberdeen. There wasn't a sandbar to speak of, just sharp rocks the water lapped against. She couldn't tell if the sandbar was washed out because of the tide or if this was how it always was. "Xavier?" she called. Her voice carried across the water. "Are you here?"

The only reply was the quiet slap of the waves.

"If you are, please come out," she pleaded. "Let's talk about this. I think I deserve that much." He was here, somewhere. She could feel it. She hoped it was because of their mate bonding and not a figment of her imagination.

Keeping her lantern held aloft, she carefully walked along the beach, looking for caves that he might have hidden in. "Why is it so insane that someone might love you as you are?" Did wildlife make their homes in Scottish beach caves? If so, was it dangerous? "I was so disappointed when I found out you couldn't turn me into a dragon," she said. "I didn't want you to be alone anymore. I don't have to be a dragon for that. I can still be your mate even if I'm only a human."

She shone her lantern into the first cave she approached, but there was nothing there.

It wasn't a cave so much as a closet in the side of the cliff, too small and short to hold a human, let alone a dragon. "Is it because I'm not enough?" she continued. "Are you running away because I'm only human?" She kept walking along the beach until she reached another cave, this one deeper, its entrance larger. Its floor was recently disturbed, pebbles brushed aside in the way a dragon's tail might swish through them. Oddly shaped paw prints appeared in spots where there was more sand than rock. More than that, there was a faint glow at its opposite end, the sort a homemade torch might give off. Her heartbeat quickened. "Xavier? Are you down here?" She followed the footprints to the other end of the cave until she reached the torch.

Xavier sat huddled against the wall in his human form, a stricken look in his eyes. A torch made from driftwood burned in a hole in the wall, its flame dying.

"Oh, thank God." Arabella set the lantern aside and crouched down next to him. "Are you all right? I've been worried sick!"

His voice was ragged. "Arabella…"

"Why the hell would you do that?" She sat in front of him, deliberately blocking his path out of the cave. "Why would you run away when I told you something good?"

"Is it?" His angry shout bounced off the walls. "I really am a monster. I've done something terrible to you. I—"

"No." She pressed her finger against his lips, silencing him. His eyes widened in surprise, but he didn't speak. "You didn't. I knew what I was in for when I hauled you aboard my dirigible in Antarctica. I knew I was getting tangled up with a dragon and I'm not willing to disentangle myself now. I think that mate bite thing is the whole reason I found you tonight at all." She remembered the baroness's help. "Well, Adelle started me in the right direction."

"What happens when you realize what I've done?" he asked hoarsely. "I've tied you to me forever. I—"

This had to be the stupidest reason to run away that she ever heard. "Yes, we're tied to each other forever. There are other ways that can happen, too. What if I'm pregnant?"

Xavier stiffened, eyes wide. "What?"

"It's an example. If I had a baby, we'd be stuck together anyway. It isn't as though we've taken precautions, so it could happen."

He ran his hand through his hair. "Christ, Arabella, I hadn't thought of that."

"Obviously not. It doesn't matter if it's a mate mark or a baby, we're still bound together." Her voice softened. "You wouldn't have done it if I wasn't your mate. It's a thing werewolves have. We assume dragons do, too. It's because you love me. I love you, too." She rose to her full height, then held out her hand but he didn't move. "You can't keep running whenever you're frightened about your dragon," she said. "You've already learned how to live with this. You're getting better at it."

"You said you wished I turned you into one." He turned beseeching eyes to her.

"I did, if it meant you wouldn't have to be alone anymore. Even if I'm still human, you aren't on your own again. I'm not leaving you."

Xavier finally stood up and gave her a look that pulled at her heart. "I know you mean that."

Hope flared in her heart. "Of course, I do. I would never lie to you. Both of us are too odd to function in polite society. We may as well be odd together."

"As long as I'm not running away again, promise me something."

She nodded. "Anything." Relief poured through her at his change of heart, his reassurance that he was willing to give what she knew they could have together a fair shot.

He pressed his forehead against hers, breath ragged. "Promise me you'll never fly an ornithopter at night in unfamiliar skies and then wander around a cliff side in the dark. Both of them are incredibly dangerous."

That was what he was worried about? "I promise."

"I'm not even considering the added danger of doing those things when it's a full moon and you're surrounded by werewolves."

"I was with Adelle. She wanted to fly in the ornithopter."

"My God." He looked at her like she was insane. "You took the wife and baroness of a werewolf leader in that death trap?"

"We were all right." Arabella didn't tell him about the baroness being sick over the side of the basket.

He shook his head. "Just… promise me you won't do these foolish things again."

215

"What about another journey to Antarctica?" She thought of his glittering lair, all the things he'd had to leave behind. She wondered if he missed them.

"No. I'll tie you to the bed first."

Arabella felt herself blush. "You would?"

He flinched.

"I wouldn't mind it if you did," she said. She reached for his shoulders, sliding her palms over his skin. "In fact, while we're here and you're already naked…"

"Not in a cave. These aren't safe." There was a catch in his voice, like he wished it wasn't the case. A few stones shook themselves loose from their moorings on the wall, as if to articulate Xavier's point. "We need to get out of here," he announced. Grasping her hand, he led her out of the cave as pebbles rained down around them. A larger rock dislodged itself when they crossed the cave mouth, landing with a wet plop on the ground. "I would never look for fossils in these caves. They're unstable."

"Then why did you hide out in them?"

"I didn't know where else to go. I just flew until I reached the water."

"Would you have come back to me at the manor?"

He looked at her, then at the water. "I don't know. I was so panicked when you told me what the bite meant and I thought I'd ruined your life."

"Stop." She placed a hand against his cheek. He leaned in to her as he did in his dragon form at the bedroom window. "You didn't. Every day since I crashed into your mountain has been an adventure and *I* was the one who ruined *your* life."

He clasped her hand and brought it to his lips. "You did no such thing. I could've left your dirigible if I really wanted to. I could have schemed my way aboard another expedition back in Santiago. But I couldn't bear the idea of not being with you, even if it meant returning to England." He pressed his forehead against hers. "I love you so much, Arabella."

She kissed him, wrapping her arms around his neck and putting everything she could into it. His response was immediate, and she thought she might have changed his mind about staying on the beach a little longer. A wave splashed them, soaking her boots and trousers.

"It feels like it's going to rain," Xavier announced. "We should get out of here. Let me shift and I'll take you up the cliff."

"Really?" She remembered the last time she sat astride his back when they were still in Antarctica. She hadn't had a chance to truly enjoy the experience.

"What's the use in being a dragon if I can't carry my love on my back once in a while?"

In a moment, he stood on the beach on all fours, scales shining in the moonlight. He snuffled the rocky beach, some smoke issuing from his nostrils, then crouched so his belly nearly touched the ground.

Arabella steeled herself and climbed on his back, grasping his shoulders for support.

Rain lightly misted them as they rose in the air and she leaned against him, feeling his heartbeat course through his body. Above the beach, he roared. A bright ball of flame exploded over the rocks, a declaration of his love.

EPILOGUE

*G*reaves Estate, Arabella's ancestral family home, wasn't as unsettling and weird as she led Xavier to believe. Or perhaps he found it charming because of Arabella's presence.

The surrounding village of Gull's End was a whole other matter, however. They had taken a couple of trips into it for supplies since they arrived and found the hospitality somewhat... lacking, to put it mildly. It seemed the village thought the house was cursed. Xavier and Arabella living together without being married also added to the stigma but neither of them cared. What mattered was they were together, in a home of their own of sorts. It even had its own small bowling alley.

It was Arabella's first visit to the estate since its extensive renovations over a year ago, during Lucien Quinn's disastrous tenancy. When she gave Xavier a tour of the house, she pointed out the newly constructed wall that replaced the doorway that once led to the house's underwater ballroom, now gone. "At least it will make this place easier to sell," she said. "I don't know what my ancestors were thinking with that stupid room." But she wasn't planning on selling the estate for a while. It was nice, she explained, to stay in one spot for a few months. Once they grew bored of the estate, they would board the dirigible, now anchored on the property, and take to the skies for somewhere new to explore.

What mattered to Xavier was the manner of all kinds of sparkling and shiny things the house had. He could hoard and hide to his dragon heart's content. The silverware collection was of particular interest, and would be coming with them when they eventually left.

Xavier's life changed once again on an unseasonably warm Sunday afternoon in early October. He'd spent the morning at the property's pebbled beach, looking for interesting rocks to add to a growing collection he kept outside the servants' door off the kitchen. Arabella found him barefoot, with water up to his ankles, an unreadable expression on her face.

"Xavier?" She looked a little pale and unsure of herself, both out of character for her.

Something in her voice had every sense of his on alert. His dragon stirred, wanting to know what was wrong with his mate. "What is it?"

Arabella looked at the water, at a loss for words for possibly the first time in her life.

His heartbeat thundered so hard he thought she must be able to hear it. "What's wrong?" he repeated.

"Would you marry me?"

He was so taken aback by the question that he nearly fell over. "What?"

"Would you marry me?" she repeated. She opened her palm to reveal a pair of freshly cleaned ruby earbobs, an old-fashioned set if he'd ever seen them. They had to be older than the house itself. Damn it if his dragon didn't want to snatch them out of her hand and hide them away in his trouser pocket.

"A ring may be more traditional," she said.

"I believe *my* asking *you* would be more traditional."

"I think I'm pregnant."

Well, that wasn't what Xavier was expecting to hear. *Is it?* a small voice reminded him. *How long did you think you keep up what you were doing without this happening?* Xavier didn't care. Once the shock had worn off, delight crept in. "Are you certain?"

"I think so. The symptoms I've been having for the last couple of weeks couldn't be anything else." That unnerved, unsure look returned to her face. He hated to see it. "Is that all right?"

He was affronted that she would ask. "Of course!"

"It's such a change for both of us, and…"

He silenced her with a kiss. "I want this and I think I would have married you as soon as I set foot in England again, looking back on it."

A relieved smile spread across her face. "Why not New York?"

"Why not Santiago? It would've been that much faster." He traced the outline of her cheek with his fingertips. She sighed, leaning into his touch.

"I want to be with you," he continued. "For the rest of my life. I love you so much."

"I love you, too." She wrapped her arms around him and rested her head on his shoulder. "Although I should tell you that I'm terrified of being a parent, even though I wanted to be one eventually."

"So am I. I'm sure our baby will be, too. We'll be terrified together." He liked how the words "our baby" sounded, just as much as "together."

"Promise me one thing," Arabella said.

"Anything."

"Let it stay a secret between us that I asked you to marry me."

Xavier stepped out of the water to the beach and picked her up. She squealed and grabbed his shoulders. "I'll do one better." His teeth grazed her ear, sending a shudder of pleasure through her body. "I'll propose to you properly instead."

"When?"

"Let me look through my hoard." He started walking back to the house with her in his arms. "And I'll find a ring."

～

8 November 1888

MY DEAREST ARABELLA,

While we were disappointed to hear that you and your husband decided against a proper wedding and eloped instead, I'm still delighted to see you settled down. At least, your idea of settling down.

I hope you and Xavier enjoy your honeymoon at Greaves Manor. I'm flummoxed that you would choose such a place to start your married life, but if it makes you happy, then I'm pleased for you.

Our invitation still stands to visit us in Torquay whenever you want.

Love always,
Your father

～

20 November 1888

DEAR FATHER,

I cannot imagine how our ancestors fared in this godawful place the villagers call Gull's End, but at least Greaves Manor is interesting. Xavier has been keeping busy looking for fossils of ancient ferns or some such long-extant plant.

Speaking of ancestors, I suppose all of us will be such people to our next generation. Xavier and I anticipate meeting ours in the early spring.

Much love,
Arabella

ABOUT THE AUTHOR

Jessica Marting is a sci-fi and paranormal romance author, art enthusiast (not quite an artist, despite all that time in art school), an avid reader, and makeup collector. She lives in Toronto.